HIJABISTAN

Sabyn Javeri is an award-winning short-story writer and a novelist. She is a professor of literature and creative writing in Pakistan. Her first novel, *Nobody Killed Her*, was published by HarperCollins in 2017.

Praise for *Nobody Killed Her*

'Sabyn shuns the idea of playing victim ... Her narrative breaks the tradition of the rich lyrical accounts that emerge from the continent that largely recounted women's stories from the victim's perspective.'

– Firstpost

'Sabyn Javeri's debut novel tackles some uncomfortable truths around women, power and ambition.'

– *The Indian Express*

'It connected me with ... how difficult political journeys are for women in our subcontinent, how sham our democracies are, how deeply entrenched patriarchy is, how fanaticism is unleashed in its many shades.'

– *Hindustan Times*

HIJABISTAN

Stories

SABYN JAVERI

HarperCollins *Publishers* India

First published in India by
HarperCollins *Publishers* in 2019
A-75, Sector 57, Noida, Uttar Pradesh 201301, India
www.harpercollins.co.in

2 4 6 8 10 9 7 5 3 1

P-ISBN: 978-93-5302-902-9
E-ISBN: 978-93-5302-688-2

Typeset in 11.5/14.5 Warnock Pro at
Manipal Digital Systems, Manipal

Printed and bound at
Thomson Press (India) Ltd

For Ami
Please forgive me...

Contents

The Date

If you had peeked in through the dusty, grey windows only a few minutes earlier, you would have seen a middle-aged man and a young woman struggling with each other. You would not be wrong in thinking the man was trying to climb on to the wriggling girl. But no, it wasn't what you think it was. He wasn't particularly forceful and she not really shy. What was taking place was actually in custom with what tradition demanded. A girl should not give her body away too easily and a man should show a bit of force. And so they went back and forth, tussling and tossing, each knowing in their heart of hearts that this was a mere formality. Like any other transaction in this part of the world, sex outside of marriage too had its norms which had to be observed.

But now the two bodies lay still in the shadowy Karachi flat. One pale as ivory, the other like melting dark chocolate, both breathing heavily. Every now and then, the noise of a motorcycle roaring past or the sound of a rickshaw spluttering along the lane outside punctuated the silence, but it did nothing to stir the immobile bodies that lay still, like scattered pieces of a broken earthen pitcher. Each lost in their own thoughts, each reflecting on the terms of the transaction.

The transaction, or 'the date', as the girl liked to think of it, had begun with a question. A question that the girl now thought was more of an assumption, for it really could not be answered any other way but with a yes. If you were to ask her how it happened, she would have said it all began with a new scarf. You see, it had been only a few months since she had joined the man's workforce and, that day, he had called her into his glass cabin. She knew she had been punctual and hard-working and had no reason to fear, yet felt a rising panic grip her throat as she pushed open the glass door.

Smoothing her dupatta over her head and holding it close to her skin, she stood waiting. When he pretended not to see her, she cleared her throat. 'Yes, sir?' she asked with some trepidation in her voice.

The man leaned back in his chair, the creaking of the faux leather under his bulk reminding her of a series of small farts.

'Come in, please.'

She looked up, surprised to hear his voice which was strangely seductive and husky, unlike his looks which she had found repulsive and reptilian.

'The manager was saying your mother is unwell?'

'Sir ...' she began, but lost her words to a wave of embarrassment. She felt herself blush, for the sick mother had been an excuse to leave early the past few days.

Perhaps he mistook her silence for grief or maybe he knew her kind only too well. But whatever the reason, he asked her if she would like an advance on her salary.

The girl had left his glass cubicle with immense relief and just a little spark of excitement.

In the coming days, he called her in many times. Mostly to ask about her mother and then about her own life. Was she married, where did she live, did she like working here ... The girl was only too happy to get away from the blank glare of the computer and the oppressive heat of the overhead fan into his air-conditioned office. Till one day, he asked her if she would like to meet him outside of work.

And then the man had, as if to answer his own question, pushed a small square box – wrapped in shiny silver paper and adorned with an elaborate bow – across his expansive chipboard-and-formica desk, towards her. He did not look at her. And she did not look away from the present. There were very few occasions in her life when she had received gifts, and this overly shiny, glitzy wrapped box appealed to her. Without accepting it outright, she began a guessing game in her head.

A perfume, some chocolate, jewellery?

The man leaned back in his chair, finally glancing up at her. He seemed to be guessing her reaction. Given her non-designer cotton shalwar-kameez with the white chiffon dupatta wound loosely around her hennaed hair and patchy bleached skin, whitened unevenly by local fairness creams, he seemed confident that she would accept his proposition. This was despite the fact that in the past there had been one or two young women, of the same class and background, who had chosen to take the moral high ground. He recalled now how most of the receptionists who came to work for him had some sort of a sixth sense as to what was required, but there had been a few who had pretended not to understand him and left without notice.

He narrowed his eyes, watching her watch the gift. No, she was not their kind. There was something about the way this woman stared for hours at the blank screen of her computer, stirring only when the phones rang. A break-up or an unrequited love or perhaps some trouble at home, he mused. But whatever it was, if she was searching for something to fulfil her dreams, he would help her.

He sat up suddenly and she stepped back instinctively. Gingerly, he placed his hand on the shiny silver square. Her eyes travelled all the way from the box to the hair covering the back of his hand to the gold of the watch peeking out from beneath his stiff white cuffs, up the length of his short arm, narrow shoulders, thick neck, and to the round, almost football-like head that sat stiffly on his shoulders.

He smiled crookedly.

She looked away, a dizzying wave overcoming her. What surprised her was not guilt, but the lack of it. Why wasn't she revolted? Where was the disgust? Instead, she felt the prick of excitement, as if she was about to embark on a thrilling adventure.

He lifted the lid of the box and pulled out a beautiful silk scarf. 'For you,' he said.

The fabric was embellished with faux gems and she was enthralled. But at the same time, her brow furrowed. It was a headscarf.

'A beautiful girl like you should be hidden from prying eyes.'

His words seemed to thaw whatever ice had formed at seeing the piece of cloth, instead of the perfume or jewellery she had imagined. She saw herself through his eyes. A little voice in her head kept repeating, 'beautiful girl'. She saw herself as she imagined he did – attractive, fair-skinned, delicate, decent. At this, her thoughts halted momentarily as she wondered what her favourite heroine in the TV dramas she watched regularly, would do. The tune of *Humsafer* played in her mind and she was reminded of the drama's overly pious and sacrificial heroine, but she dismissed the thought as she remembered the actress Mahira's smoking habit – something she was unapologetic about despite public outrage. *Mahira would do the same*, the woman told herself as she picked up the box. She hid the box in the folds of her dupatta wordlessly.

The man's smile widened. 'You're welcome,' he whispered to her, retreating back.

It began innocently enough, with drop-offs near home and coffees at the mall. The only change that people around her noticed was that she had started wearing the headscarf he had given her in a tightly wound hijab, and complimented it with a long abaya that she took off only when she was inside the office. Perhaps some part of her wanted to be hidden from the rest of the world, like the secret inside her. But to her family, she said it was because people harassed her on public transport. The family, in turn, was only too glad that she had embraced the right path.

The right path had many deviations, mostly in the form of dimly lit restaurants and secluded parks. The day came when they met at a Chinese restaurant off Tariq Road, where they ate greasy chowmein in the eerie red light of a dimly lit corner. After that, they walked quietly to his small car and got in. She noticed he didn't turn on the AC. To outsiders, they seemed like any other married couple.

That day, he invited her to a friend's flat. She was smart enough to know what it meant, naïve enough to know what it didn't.

In the partly furnished flat, he offered her a bracelet. It was nothing valuable, yet she felt a wave of gratitude wash over her. 'He cares,' she heard a voice repeat over and over in her head. She knew he was married. She knew he knew she wasn't. And she knew what it meant. But still, she was willing to risk it. She did not know why. She dared not ask herself why. Perhaps she had never learnt to question in the first place.

He managed to get her to lie down on the narrow slated bed. And as she looked with feigned interest at the frayed frame of the rusty glass window, he peeled away her clothes. She lay limp, like a newborn, stifling all desire and displaying only a bored disinterest to what was happening to her body. Once he was inside her, she seemed to relax and he thrust hard.

'No,' she cried, struggling against him, and he looked up at her in surprise.

With great effort, as he slowed to a stop, he asked, 'Do you really want me to stop?'

She looked at his sweaty face, his eyes half-moons, and shook her head. He buried his face in her breast and thrust twice more before collapsing on her like a dead crab. From below, she watched his small body splattered over her. She prodded him gently.

'Shall I turn over?' she asked, slightly annoyed at how abruptly the greatly anticipated adventure was over.

If he was surprised at her words, he didn't show it. With an almost Herculean effort, he raised himself up on his elbows and she turned over, her hips staring up at him like two brown mole hills. He was not aroused. Like a ticker at the bottom of a news channel, a thought kept running through his mind: *This is not her first time.*

'What happened?' the girl's muffled voice broke into his thoughts.

He looked down at her face pressed into the pillow, her hips thrusting up at him invitingly, and willed himself to feel something. But all he could see now was the creeping cellulite, the stark contrast of dark against light on her dimply skin, rough at some places and scaly at others. He gently turned her over. What stared up at him put him off even more. He peered closely and noticed what he had missed in his excitement earlier.

'I'm sorry,' he heaved.

The girl stared at him. He looked to her like an injured wolf.

Embarrassed, he grabbed his thigh and began to massage it vigorously. 'Think I've pulled a muscle,' he groaned in fake pain that did little to convince her. Both knew that the moment had passed.

Annoyed, she pushed him aside. *She* didn't expect it to be his first time, she thought bitterly, realizing exactly what it was that was hurting her much-married boss. She sat up and grabbed her clothes from where he had tossed them on the floor. She watched him stare at her as she wriggled into them as discreetly as she could. She knew what he was looking at.

Finally, the man could not contain himself any longer and said, 'You have hair.'

She looked down at the thatch between her legs and stood stickily with her feet apart.

'Yes,' she said matter-of-factly.

He looked at her headscarf, tossed ruthlessly on to the floor when they first began kissing, then back at her pubic hair.

'But ... but it is not pious.'

For a second, she was stunned at this assumption of her piety. Had he really forgotten that the scarf was *his* gift, she thought with a rising annoyance. She thought she heard him mutter something about making an honest woman out of her and, suddenly, the absurdity of the whole situation struck her.

She threw back her head and laughed so loudly that for a moment he felt frightened of this little creature that had let out a laugh as ferocious as a lion's roar. He was reminded of the time when, once, he had taken his kids to the zoo and they had seen a lioness open her mouth and yawn. It had seemed to him like some sort of soundless laugh and he had felt in that moment as if he were being mocked. He felt it again now, with her uproarious laughter ringing in the tiny room.

'It is,' she said in between mouthfuls of suffocating laughter. Feeling the weight of his gaze on her, she willed herself to stop. She turned away, a clownish smile still plastered on her face, as she struggled to tie her bra. With a sacrificial sigh, he got up to help her and she instinctively pulled away. She wasn't sure why she did that, but knew that this scrutiny of his had sprung up some sort of distance between them.

In a softer tone, she said, 'I can do it myself.'

He remained silent but she thought she saw a hint of a smirk.

'But,' she said as she pushed her hands through the sleeves of her long kurta, 'you shouldn't make assumptions, you know.'

'I wasn't,' he said as he handed her the scarf.

She paused before taking it in. She found herself wondering if he agreed with her or if he really believed her to be someone she had never claimed to be.

She opened her mouth to say something, but he looked away. Like a fish trying to breathe, she opened and closed her mouth, wondering if he wanted her to leave. As if to quietly send the message across, he glanced purposefully at his watch.

She wanted at that moment to hit him. But she couldn't. He was her boss.

To keep her hands busy, she started buttoning her abaya, the long string of buttons demanding her focus.

'So tell me,' he said, leaning back against a pillow and lighting a cigarette. 'You wear an abaya, a hijab, you probably pray five times a day, but you don't remove your pubic hair? I mean ...' He let out a long slow exhale and continued, 'Isn't that impure? Napak? Against Sunnah? What is that Hadith? Hair should not be longer than a grain of rice ...' He paused and then suddenly, realizing the irony of the situation, began to laugh. Watching his sheepish laughter, she too was reminded of an animal. Except to her, the shrill pitch of his laugh was reminiscent of a hyena.

She smoothed the folds of her abaya and stepped in front of the floor-length mirror. Slowly, she raised her waist-length hair to the top of her head in a topknot, then began to tie her hijab around it. Then came the sunglasses. And in a moment, she had transformed into just about any other woman on the streets of Karachi, making her way home after a hard day's work, plodding away at a mundane, office job.

Addressing him through the mirror, she said, 'It's uncomfortable.'

But the man had moved on. He was going through his phone, his thumb furiously texting, messaging, his eyes scrolling up and down the screen.

'I said—' she began, then stopped mid-sentence. Instead, she looked at him through the mirror. In that moment, as the man on the bed scrolled through his phone, he seemed no different from any other man. She tore her eyes away from him and stared at her own reflection. It seemed to be mocking her.

'Why am I doing this?' she whispered to herself. Looking at him again, she took in his sunken chest, his protruding stomach. The thick reading glasses resting on his even thicker nose, and the deep brown of his skin almost merging with the mahogany of the eyeglasses. But it wasn't his looks that repelled her. It was his indifference that bothered her.

And in that moment, she knew why.

He made her feel wanted. Even if only for a few minutes.

And now, as she tugged her hijab into place and picked up her bag, she thought with affectionate pity that it was sweet of him. It was sweet of him to think she dressed modestly and probably prayed five times. It was sweet of him to think ... to think that she was pious. Pure.

She pulled up the folds of the hijab across her mouth and nostrils and thought how in this aspect he was like her family. They too had been pleasantly surprised when she started wearing the hijab and the abaya. They too had thought her pious.

'Let them,' she whispered to herself as she crossed the distance across the rug, from the mirror to the bed.

She sat down at the edge and gently pulled his phone away.

'I'm leaving now.'

He nodded indulgently and pulled out his wallet.

'For the taxi,' he said.

She hesitated before taking it. It was almost as if he were putting a price on it. *Better a price than a name,* she thought firmly as she took in the money five times the cost of a taxi ride back.

'He cares about me,' she told herself as she shut the door behind her. 'He cares a lot.' She counted the money and stuffed it quickly into her purse before boarding the bus, a part of her knowing that her services were no longer needed.

On the bus, she camouflaged herself amidst the other veiled women, all shrinking into themselves, willing their bodies to become invisible and unfeeling to the pinching and groping that no number of hijabs and burkhas seemed to deter.

Ten minutes before her stop, she texted her younger brother to meet her at the bus stop. And he was there, probably nagged by her mother, blackmailed into helping his sister who, crippled by her gender, was helpless in walking home alone.

She stepped off the bus behind three other abaya-clad ladies, and almost burst into raucous laughter again as her brother approached the woman in front of her and called her 'Api'.

The woman ignored him and her brother seemed embarrassed.

'You all look the same,' he grumbled. 'In this sea of black burkhas, I can't tell who is who.'

She frowned as she mounted the motorbike her fifteen-year-old brother was allowed to ride but was off limits to her. As they sped through the narrow lanes and dug-up roads towards the airless cement cage they called home, she looked in the bike's side mirrors and watched the road behind them disappear in a haze of grey exhaust smoke. She smiled. The sunglasses were the first to go, then the headscarf, which she tugged at till it came loose. She spent the rest of the bumpy ride feeling the breeze on her face and scalp, and thinking about how she would spend the money.

The Urge

It all began the day they put the all-encompassing dark garment on me. It was a passage to womanhood, they said. Now that I was older, I must wear a hijab. And an abaya too. I must be good. A good Muslim. A good, Muslim, woman.

I had just turned thirteen.

'Here.' They held it out to me as if it were a prize. And perhaps it was. I tried on the patterned headscarf and the long, black, cloak-like garment that covered me like a tent.

I felt hidden.

'You are lucky,' Amma told me later that day. 'Nowadays, girls in Pakistan get away with so much. In our days, it was a baggy shuttlecock burkha thrown over our heads, with just a few tiny holes to peer through. And then, before we could even learn to walk without tripping on the hem, we were packed off to the husband's house.'

I fingered the silky material of the abaya. It was smooth, like the chocolates an uncle had once brought us from Jeddah.

Amma seemed to be thinking the same thoughts, for she said, 'Aye, you remember that beautiful silk your uncle got us from Saudi?'

I nodded, though only the sweets had remained stuck in my memory.

'I had it made from that material only.'

'Oh.' I don't know why, but I felt a sudden pang. The smoothness of the fabric was sensuous. It seemed as if this thing really did have chocolates woven into its texture. I had a sudden urge to taste it.

I put it in my mouth.

'Chi! Acting like a baby,' Amma snatched it from my mouth. 'Why I wasted such a fine cloth from Saudi on you! Ya Allah, have mercy.' Lamenting, she made her way to the kitchen.

I thought back to the TV show where I'd heard some short-haired women, who looked like boys, tch-tching at the Saudis for not letting women drive. I wondered if that too was a bad thing.

'Amma,' I began, but she was already at the stove. 'Amma,' I called out, 'they don't let women drive in Saudia.'

'So?' she shouted back. 'It's because they don't make their women work like these blasted Pakistani men who make us fetch the water, work the fields, do the bazaars and what not. And where did you hear it anyway? Have you *been* to Saudi? Don't let women drive! One less chore it is for us women, if you ask me!'

Not that we have *a car*, I thought, checking the deep pockets of the abaya. I held it up against the sunlight and thought a few metal buttons on the edge would definitely do. I got out Amma's sewing box and began sewing an assortment of different coloured buttons along the edge. I worked quickly, secretly, keeping one eye on the doorway, should Amma make a sudden reappearance. But I knew it would be a while before she left the stove. She cooked with great concentration and as a result, Amma's food always tasted exactly the same.

Was that a good thing? I found myself wondering for the second time that day.

'You are not secretly watching those vulgar Indian channels with the volume down, are you?' Amma called out from the kitchen. I pricked my finger at the sudden sound of her voice. 'If your uncle catches you, both you and I will get a good thrashing.'

'No!' I cried out, the thought of my holier-than-thou uncle's relentless slaps blinding my thoughts. 'No. I ... I'm just looking at the hijab.' I watched as the blood from my finger seeped onto the abaya, then disappeared into its inky blackness. I wondered if it would stain but, no, the dark material seemed to absorb everything inside it. Very carefully, I put the hijab on my head the way Amma had taught me, then wrapped myself in the long, dark hold of the abaya. Something shifted. I looked up to see a lizard on the wall, staring unblinkingly at me.

'It's still me,' I whispered. She seemed unconvinced, so I ran inside for a quick look. In the small, scratched, rusted mirror hung high on the bedroom wall, I stared at my reflection. Someone else stared back at me. Not a girl of thirteen, but a dark, mysterious woman. This was someone else, I thought.

This was a woman.

At first, I enjoyed the freedom the hijab offered. Inside the tent-like abaya, I could be scratching my crotch or unbutton the annoying bra I was forced to wear. Nobody could tell. It was, in some ways, like travelling in your own private marquee. I felt sheltered. Nobody told me not to fidget or to sit still, nobody said good girls don't pick their noses or scratch their bums, because nobody could tell what I was up to in there. I often wondered if all women did this. How sorry I felt for the menfolk, whose freedom I had envied so much previously. They stood there in the hot sun, so exposed, so raw, so open, doing their business with everyone watching. So many times I had seen men standing on the sidewalk, scratching their crotch in full view of the public or squatting shamelessly on the sidewalks, their limp penis in their hand as they finished peeing. I used to envy their freedom to do what they liked, when they liked, no worries as to who might be watching. Now I pitied them. *Poor deprived souls*, I thought.

But then, like most things that one gets used to, this too got boring. I began to miss my colourful clothes. I missed stealing glances at my reflection in shop mirrors and the thrill of getting compliments. There was no longer any point in trying out new hairstyles or haircuts. Even brushing my hair seemed pointless, for there was no one to see it. No one to compliment or to complain –

nobody to notice me at all. I could go out in rags for all I cared; it hardly mattered unless I was going somewhere I could take off my camouflage and stand out.

And that was rare. Even at weddings, unless they were segregated, I had to wear the cumbersome garment.

It was a woman's fate, I was told.

Make the best of it, I was ordered.

I had heard somewhere that necessity is the mother of invention. In my case, it was the aunt. I tried inventing new games to make life in purdah interesting, and young Aunt, my uncle's new wife, a girl just six years older than me, joined in. We often played dress-up with her still-new wedding clothes, putting on what little make-up and jewels she had, for a make-believe wedding. We loved make-up, but Uncle called it the devil's opium, throwing away any cosmetics he found on our person.

'Good girls don't dirty their faces,' he warned us, smoothing his long black beard as he quoted some ominous Arabic verse or the other.

But nobody knew what his Arabic verses meant so we did what we had to behind his back.

Once, in a departmental store, Aunt and I saw a red lipstick. It was fire engine red, too beautiful to pass up. It beckoned me, called out to me, *urged* me to pick it up. I could imagine my aunt's reaction if I asked her to buy it for me. She had never worn such a bright colour in her life. But that is not what would stop her. The bigger never-been-done-before factor here was that we'd never bought anything from this store. It wasn't just the fact that she had no money; even if she did, it was the feeling of guilt – as if we weren't supposed to be there. To be honest, I'm not sure how she even wrangled the permission. Or why. She brought me here on Sundays when Uncle took the whole family to the promenade for a stroll. I never found out how she persuaded him to let us go. She always insisted that he drop us off here, taking me along as an escort, and my younger brother as guardian. She was still childless, you see, and my mother, with six children to look after, was only too happy to have a few off her plate. But I digress, my youngish aunt, with whom my much older uncle was totally besotted, would somehow convince him to drop us off at the mall by the sea and here, under the bright lights and loud store music, we'd browse the colourful merchandise, dawdling in the fairness creams section, marvelling at the whitening potions and, of course, staring in fascination at the Revlon Red counter – knowing fully well that we could never afford any of it.

It was not the first time I had gaped at the red lipstick, marvelling at its power of transformation as the ugly sales girl tried it on. Nor was it the first time the thought of stealing it had occurred to me. But earlier, there had been no opportunity. A girl of eleven, with no handbag and only her slim kurta-pyjama, has nothing but a fist to hide things in. But a girl in a hijab has much more opportunity.

And so, that day, I gave in to the urge. And why not? I asked myself. The hijab is a garment that implies purity. Who would think of looking under it? What security guard would risk frisking a girl wearing such a holy garment? Why would such a girl steal? Would *you*?

That night, I took it out of the folds of my long abaya and there it gleamed, the red devil. I felt seduced. Fire-engine siren, it read. I giggled and stayed longer than usual in the bathroom I shared with my family of ten, my brothers threatening to break down the door if I didn't come out soon. When I finally emerged, Amma and Aunt averted their eyes, but after dinner, they sat me down.

I wondered if some telltale red sign had remained on my mouth despite the vigorous scrubbing. Did they know?

My mother cleared her throat while my aunt looked uncomfortable, adjusting her headscarf nervously. Finally, Amma pressed a small book of holy verses into my hands.

'Beti,' she said, 'when a girl reaches puberty, the body is not the only thing that needs sheltering. It is not just the appearance that must be hidden from preying eyes. One must protect the mind as well. If you ...' her voice trailed off. Aunt looked shiftily from side to side, looking more and more uncomfortable as Amma's face took on a stoic look and her voice acquired the tone of a martyr.

'Look, beti,' Amma said in a low, pleading tone, 'if you get the urge ... the urge to ... oh you will know what I mean ... you know if you feel you must remain longer in the bathroom...'

I sighed with relief. So this was what it was about. Did she really think that sharing a room with my five siblings and sexually overactive parents had not taught me anything? Besides, the girls at the madrassa had already told me about it, some of us even discussing techniques, debating whether one finger or two fingers were more effective.

I decided to put an end to her misery.

'Amma, I will say my prayers when the need arises. Thank you.' I bowed my head like a dutiful daughter. They looked visibly relieved.

I ran out of the room, my fingers touching the reassuring presence of the fire-engine red, then travelling south as I wondered, *Did they really start that late?*

The urge, I noticed with time, could appear in many forms at different places and disguises. My urges were not physical, as my mother and aunt had feared, but material. Soon, I found it was harder and harder not to give in to them. If I spotted a juicy red apple, my hands itched to grab it and hide it in the folds of my abaya. If I saw Uncle's keys, I just couldn't stop myself from tucking them into my hijab, if for nothing else than to see his face twist into rage as he hunted desperately for them.

But as I grew older, the urge began to manifest itself in different ways. Every time I saw Indian film stars on cable, I wanted to look like them.

'As long as you do your fashion inside your hijab,' Aunt, who seemed to experience the same urges, warned me. She taught me how to. It became a secret game between us. We cut off the sleeves of our old shirts and pretended to be wearing western dresses under our abayas. We giggled at the thought that nobody knew how immodestly we were dressed underneath. One day I saw an old Hindi film where the actress sang a sad song wearing a one-shouldered dress and had an uncontrollable urge to tear away my own sleeve. Aunt stopped me, instead snipping away the whole shoulder of an old kameez, making it a one-strap dress like the kind the Indian actress had worn. I made her try it on, too.

She resisted at first, but finally gave in. When she stepped out from behind the curtain we used for changing, she looked different. Her heavy breasts bulged against the ill-fitting, lopsided neckline, her face contorted with shyness. I took out the red lipstick and coloured her lips.

'There,' I said. 'Smile,' I commanded, and she smiled. 'Walk.' 'Turn.' Before I knew it, she was making poses and pretending to do the catwalk like those tall, tall models on TV. We laughed and we laughed, and finally we collapsed on the floor. Suddenly, I stopped laughing and looked at her. Something passed between us in that moment. I reached out and touched her breasts. She didn't shy away. I let my hand explore her skin, a strange urge inside driving us closer.

Perhaps it would have led to something more, but just then, my uncle came home. We froze at the sound of his keys and, before we could cover ourselves, he was in the doorway, taking in the butchered garments, the red-stained lips, and finally my hand on her breast.

'Get out,' he ordered.

That night, her face matched the violet of her dress. But what could anyone do. *It was her fate.*

I was not allowed to enter Aunt's room again. Uncle called her a bad influence. All outings alone with her were banned. Slowly, the family visits to the seaside also came to a stop. The city's situation, the bomb blasts and the shootings made it impossible to step out. And even when things got better, it was only as far as down the lane to a cousin's home and back that I was allowed to venture. My outings were curbed more and more with each passing birthday. Finally, on my fifteenth birthday, I was imprisoned in the house. A suitable match was being sought and I was to be married soon. Till then, I was expected to bide my time learning the art of cooking and the craft of sewing. Both things bored me to tears.

If I protested, my mother and aunt would tell me to be patient. 'It's a woman's fate,' they would say in unison, like a pair of parrots. 'Once you are married, you can do what you want.'

Looking at their wistful pinched faces, I doubted it, but I consoled myself with the fact that my fate would be different. I always found a way, you see.

In the coming days, the smell of fried onions dominated my senses, needles pricked my thumbs, the scraping of meat made me nauseous, and the cumbersome peeling of potatoes made me scream. When it all got too much, I knew I had to find a way out. And that was when I found a new game.

This time, the urge was the strongest it had ever been. I began to feel as if it were my master and I had no choice but to obey. I should've known that this meant trouble.

That afternoon, when everyone was asleep, I crept out to the little balcony overlooking our narrow lane. There was nobody about, except the shopkeeper opposite fanning himself with a newspaper, his pedestal fan turning slowly, miserably, airlessly. I walked up to the edge and looked down, hoping and praying that he wouldn't look up.

He did.

Before I could stop the urge, I lifted my abaya and flashed him. The shock on his face was enough to make me tremble in my skin. I covered myself quickly and ran inside, panting as if I had been chased. I was shaking. I couldn't stop. What would happen now? I had exposed myself to him. What if the man complained to my uncle? What if he went to the police? What if I was stoned to death? Thrown out for being a bad girl?

I was still trembling as I cowered in a corner of the kitchen, when my mother called out to me, 'Girl, get the afternoon tea ready. Your uncle and father will be here soon.'

Quickly, I composed myself and, putting on proper clothes under my hijab, I busied myself in the kitchen. And that is when I noticed it – we were out of sugar.

'Go with your little brother and get it on credit from across the street,' mother shouted. Precisely what I had feared.

I shivered, shouting back, 'Why can't he get it himself? He's almost four now!'

But Amma shook her head. 'He can't cross the road. Those cursed motorcycles come so fast down the alley. Just go, na. As it is, you've got your full cover on.'

My hands and feet felt dead cold and my ears were buzzing as I stepped out of our tiny house. Holding my brother's hand, I led him to the shop across the road.

'Half kilo sugar,' he said in his little squeak of a voice.

I looked up to see if the shopkeeper was leering at me but he seemed to be avoiding my gaze. *He's embarrassed*, I thought to myself, my face reddening with shame. And then, as I took the pen to sign the credit note, I felt him brush his hand against mine. I felt him linger a second too long. Something hot flashed between my legs. The top of my spine shivered.

'Let's go,' my little brother tugged at my sleeve and we left. But, as filmy as it sounds, my heart remained behind.

From that day on, it became a ritual. Sometimes a leg, sometimes a breast, or a wrist, even a flash of my buttocks. We waited eagerly for the afternoons when I would go up to the roof and tease him with my urges.

I lived in constant fear and I lived in constant excitement. At times, I couldn't tell what was greater – the risk of being found out or the satisfaction of giving in to my impulses. It was as if I had invented my own world where I made the rules. I was the queen and I was the slave. It was the best of feelings, it was the worst of them. Whatever it was, it was a high.

And then, as it often happens in the love stories on cable, mine too ended abruptly. It should have been a happy ending, for once caught, thankfully not naked, making eye contact with each other, my mother put two and two together and forced the shopkeeper to propose. He was fourteen years older than me and already married, but I didn't mind. He was after all my first love, my only love.

We were married soon enough, to the joy of my siblings who finally got some space in our overcrowded house. He put me in a separate one-room quarter, away from the prying eyes of his first family – something I cherished at first, till the loneliness set in. But like with the hijab and the abaya, the novelty soon wore off. Everything that he had desired about me turned to fear. I think he was constantly haunted by the fear that I'd flash someone else. But how could I confide this shameful confession to anyone?

The hijab was not enough for him. He made me wrap a large chadder over my hijab and abaya. He got me to swear that I would always wear a bra and a vest. Even in the sweltering hot Karachi summers, I had to don a man's vest under my clothes, and leggings under my shalwar, lest I kicked my legs and someone saw my ankles.

But mere clothes are not enough when one's mind is insecure. The body must not only be covered up, it must be locked up.

And so he began to lock me up every morning when he left the house. Soon, the windows were boarded up too, the stairway to the roof barred and door padlocked from outside. The cable was cut off. The phone disconnected.

My mother said, 'He loves you too much. He doesn't want any other man to cast eyes on you.'

Or a woman, I thought, *or a bird, a worm, an ant...*

It was in this airless darkness that my nameless daughter was born. I had no phone to ring for help. No window or balcony off which I could shout out my agony. No doorway I could run through. I lay there withering in pain, shuddering, shivering, praying to Allah for mercy.

When he finally returned home and found me lying in a pool of blood and vomit, he rushed out to get the midwife, remembering, even in this emergency, to lock the front door.

I delivered on the floor. The old midwife took the hijab I had torn off my head during labour and folded it into a triangle. Tenderly, she tucked the baby in and swaddled her tight. I was handed the parcel as if it was something repugnant.

'The first one doesn't matter,' the toothless old lady mumbled, encouraging me to put her to my breast. 'But the second-born must be a boy. Remember, a boy is a provider. A boy will bring you status. A girl is a liability.'

'A girl,' I said, the wonder in my voice making the little thing open her eyes a notch.

'Put her to your breast,' the old woman said as she wiped the soiled floor on her haunches.

I held the baby tightly. *Just born and already wrapped in a hijab*, I thought with a smile. *A thing to be hidden from the rest of the world – a man's honour but not his pride.*

I held her tight.

I still don't know if I did it consciously. All I know is that the urge consumed me. The next thing I knew, the old lady was screaming, trying to pry the baby out of my hands. I had squeezed the cloth around her too tight. She was turning blue.

'Let go,' I could hear the woman scream. 'Let her go,' she shouted as I held on harder, squeezing the hijab tight around her little body till I heard her tender bones snap.

She didn't even cry.

The voices faded. And I felt as if someone had turned off the volume on the cable. I could see the midwife's lips moving. My husband behind her. Their faces angry, their fists balled. They seemed to be moving in slow motion.

'It was her fate,' I said as the baby's neck flopped to one side.

I pulled the hijab over her tiny mouth and nostrils.

The urge, you see, was much too strong.

Radha

The monsoons had come early. Lines of rain twisting like thick ropes descended from the sky as Radha opened her front door and stepped out. Gathering the falls of her chiffon sari, she quickly ducked back inside. But it was too late. Her glance fell on her new jewel-studded golden slippers, now stained a deep brown. Her pink-painted toes peeped out from her soaked slippers and for a moment she was reminded of Qari Sahib's sermon about nail polish making ablution impure. 'Water does not touch the nails if they are painted. You remain filthy,' his voice thundered in her mind and she felt a violent shudder run through her body. 'Huh,' she snorted as she felt her skin soak in the moisture, her toes squishing against the wetness. *If Qari Sahib had ever actually worn nail polish himself,* she thought, *he'd know how little a difference it made!*

A loud rumbling noise made her look out the window to see if Chaudry Sahib's driver had finally arrived. Seeing nothing but a muddy brown sky frown back at her, she realized it wasn't a car horn or even thunder, but a cleric clearing his throat into the mosque's loudspeaker. Soon enough, she heard the distant din of the Azan. Radha's face crumpled with irritation for she had been plunged into darkness at the first hint of a raindrop, whereas the mosque always seemed to have enough electricity to blast the Azan, come hail or storm. Loud enough to wake the dead, she said, giggling at the thought of skeletons congregating. And then, just as suddenly, she stopped laughing, a deep maroon creeping up her cheeks. *What is wrong with me?* she chided herself. How could I be so disrespectful. What if Amma or Abba had heard! At the thought of her parents, Radha felt an icy grip clasp her heart. It wasn't the first time she would be letting them down. And just for a moment, she allowed herself to feel the remorse and the regret, and something else that she could not quite explain. It wasn't self-pity, nor was it nostalgia. It was, perhaps, something even stronger than emotion.

'But is there anything stronger than emotions?' she wondered aloud, a melancholic smile inching its way up the corners of her mouth. Her mood lifted at the thought, replaced by a rush of adrenalin as she glanced around her tiny flat, her eyes resting on the flat-screen TV, the sound system, the fancy lamps, the shiny Kenwood toaster and finally at the paintings on the wall. 'Ahh,' she exclaimed to herself, 'art!' Now that was something her parents could not only have never been able to afford, but never understand either. They wouldn't see the point of spending money on pictures. They were strictly utilitarian, or so the tightness of money had made them.

'But whose fault is that?' she said to herself. Abba never ventured beyond his pitiful nine-to-five and Amma never dared to get a job, not even in a school, preferring instead to whine about the shortage of money, causing Abba to die young. Even after that, her mother had preferred to live off the charity of others instead of trying to earn her own. Radha shook her head and frowned. She would never be like that. She didn't care what they thought of her. She cracked her knuckles and took a determined step forward. The same survival instinct that propels the wounded to keep moving, kicked in. She threw back her shoulders and straightened her back, as if someone were pulling at her crown with a string. Facing the mirror, she touched a few flyaway wisps of hair and patted them back into place. 'Work is work,' she told her reflection.

The rumble of thunder outside made her shiver and she wondered why she had felt the need to reassure herself like this in the first place.

Not letting herself mull over this any longer, she glanced at her wrist and grumbled, 'Where is that stupid driver of Chaudry Sahib's?' Getting no answer from the mute watch, she whipped out her mobile phone and punched in a number.

'Abdul Rahim,' she shouted, 'you bastard! Where have you gone and died now? Why is the car not at the gate? And why do you give me one-bells if you are not outside? What do you mean, you are outside? I'm standing outside, you harami! Acha, acha, coming, but if even a single strand of my hair gets wet, I'll see to it that you lose your job.'

Stuffing her phone back into her purse, she stepped out once again. The streets, still muddy and filled with water, resembled the sea at low tide. A calm sea sans waves, much like how she had been feeling before this silly boy of a driver fanned her fury. Sure enough, a car came honking down the street, barely visible and almost ghostly in the watery mist. Radha locked her front door, then stepped forward tentatively, unsure how to get across without staining the edges of her pale pink sari.

'Ruqaiyah, baji,' the driver rolled down his window and called out.

Radha had been planning to dash through the deluge to the car, but the man's words stopped her. She stood rooted to the spot, willing the man to come as close as possible to her door. Part of her feared he might splash her, and part of her felt defiant. *Let him splash even one drop at me, and if I don't get him fired, my name isn't Radha.*

But her name *wasn't* Radha. Her name was actually Ruqaiyah Begum. But she preferred the soft 'dha' sound to the harsh 'qa' of her real name. Plus, Ruqaiyah, the name given to her by her parents, reeked of the old-fashioned Urdu-speaking families of the old part of town, to which she belonged. For a second, the word 'belong' made her halt and reflect. Oblivious to the driver's honking, she savoured the word like she had savoured the falling water before her. It was a delicious word, she decided, and if it had a taste, it would taste like grapefruit – sweet at first, but with a bitter aftertaste that left one's tongue reeling.

The driver's incessant honking continued as he refused to budge an inch further. By now, the neighbours were beginning to peer out of their windows at the racket. Another complaint was all Radha needed to be evicted from her ground-floor flat, and so she hiked up her sari and trudged through the water to the nearby car. Probably feeling chastised by the concession she was making, the boy grudgingly got out of the car. He bent to open the door for her just as she gave him a push, laughing as he fell backwards into the water.

When he got back dripping wet into the car, he stared at her through the rear-view mirror. She feared it was anger that flashed in his young eyes, but as soon as he caught her eye, he winked at her. Radha ignored him.

Harami sala.

She had no time to waste on the likes of him. Not when the party that awaited her was the minister himself. It had taken great skill and time to get to a place where, even if she said so herself, her art of seduction was near perfect. She had found a way to blow her clients so that they hired her again but did not get so addicted to her that they wouldn't let her take on any other men, or worse, started talking of leaving their wives. Radha sighed. She was aware that her looks were not extraordinary, but she also realized that most men were like spoilt children who just wanted to be indulged. So she sat on her knees, cock in mouth, stroking their ego, till they coughed up the money and the semen. She had learnt early on that men cared only about pleasing themselves. But what they perhaps themselves did not know was how easy it was to please them.

She knew that it wasn't the choicest of professions, but then beggars can't be choosers, she consoled herself. If this was what life had in store for her, who was she to argue, she thought as she twirled her diamond ring. After all, it wasn't as if she had planned to choose the oldest profession in the world as her career.

Radha had been a pre-med student when she got into the business of pleasure, as her pimp called it. It was a temporary arrangement, a stopgap till she saved enough to get into med school. However, she soon realized this was not much different from medicine, healing being the purpose of both. She found sex empowering. And enabling. A few months into this line, and she was independent, both financially and emotionally, from the over-protective, close-knit, suffocating, family consisting of her widowed mother, two younger brothers and a mentally challenged sister.

And it wasn't as if she had to walk the streets. It was all very discreet, for her clients had much more to lose than her, should anything get leaked. On the face of it, she was an ad-film model selling anything from detergents to paan masala to apartments. But underneath, there was a whole network of exploitation that went on at that particular agency.

She could not remember when or how she had become a part of it. Perhaps her memory had blocked it out, but she remembered it had been an older model, a mentor, who had set up the first tryst. When her mother had decided it was more important to school her brothers than her, Radha had decided to finance her own education by getting a part-time job. A friend whose brother worked in advertising got her a job as a receptionist in a small agency. One day, when a model failed to show up, they asked her to pose for a pamphlet. It was there she had met Riaz Uncle. From the first time she met him, Radha had been impressed by the kindness in his wrinkled and faded eyes, and of course the generosity of his very deep pockets. And when an older model brought his proposition to her, she accepted without thinking. And so it was that a man she called 'Uncle' took her virginity, in return for basic things like food and education. The thought suddenly made her bitter. But it was replaced with a smile when she remembered him, sixty at that time, showering her with expensive gifts with the understanding that she saw no other. He had passed away three years later. Radha realized she missed him, the man who named her Radha.

'Get married,' her family – who had looked the other way till the gifts and the cash had flowed – had advised her after the funeral. Their concern for her future had suddenly resurfaced after her patron's death: 'Log kya kahengay?' they had chorused.

'You are twenty-six,' her mother had coaxed. 'Who would marry you if word gets out?' There was a sense of urgency, an anxiety in the household, as her mother hastily hunted for rishtas and Radha – who refused to go back to being called Ruqaiyah – remembered feeling strangely aloof, as if she no longer recognized herself. 'I feel disconnected with myself,' she would tell her mother who in turn would tell her to pray.

And that is when religion came into Radha's life. Long sermons on seeking His forgiveness, made her turn to God. She would lie in bed telling beads or spend long evenings prostrating on the prayer mat. Until one day her mother took her to a Dars by Qari Shahid, the evangelical TV host who was becoming increasingly popular at the time. At first she was just a disciple, listening to his sermons, nodding her head like a clockwork toy but with time she became so committed that she even started covering her head. She wore a hijab to cover her hair and an abaya to hide her figure, but she could not conceal the sensuousness in her eyes that men were drawn to. Though they had never spoken, she returned home one day to find a demure Qari waiting for her as he sat silently, eyes downcast, in her living room. This time there was no proposition. Instead he had brought a proposal.

It seemed the right thing to do. And so a quiet nikah was performed and she found herself a bride – no henna adorning her hands, no ornaments on her person, no music and no dances marking her special day. She winced as she remembered protesting the simplicity of the occasion to her mother. 'It's not like it's your first time,' her mother had replied bitingly. After that, Radha had left the house vowing never to return. But then promises are made to be broken.

Now, as they slowly made their way through the waterlogged streets of Karachi, Radha examined the old engagement ring on her finger. The marriage had lasted all of eight months but she still wore the ring. Not because it was precious or particularly pretty – instead, it was its coarseness that appealed to her. It was tight and slightly pinched her skin too. It was this discomfort that reminded her not to go back to her old life of domesticity, whenever a client proposed.

Qari had turned out to be a mean man, tight-fisted and insecure. He professed Wahabism, but Radha had decided he was just miserly. He kept her hand-to-mouth and, after about six months of desperation, Radha ran back home, sending him a Qula notice through her younger brother. She had feared that he would not divorce her easily, but he did. As quietly and as unceremoniously as he had proposed to her.

In the car, she wiped the mist off the windowpane, avoiding the driver's gaze, and thought back to how she had willingly started wearing the hijab to please the Qari. She touched her hair now, stroked its softness, aware that the driver was likely getting a hard-on in the front seat. Then she gently brought her hand down, resting it under her chin. With the other hand, she adjusted a stray lock, tossing it back over her plump shoulders, knowing fully well the devastation she was unleashing in the front seat.

The car halted and she felt the driver's eyes on her again. Now he really did have her full attention. To convey this, she met his eyes in the mirror. The honking around them grew louder as their eyes locked and the car remained unmoving. Without breaking the grid-locked gaze, and unbeknown to the boy, Radha's free hand reached for her mobile. It was only when she said,

'Jee, Chaudry Sahib, we are almost there,' that he stepped
on the gas and they were on their way once again. He did
not dare glance at her through the rear-view mirror for
the rest of the journey.

Radha smiled. It had taken a long time, but she
knew how to take care of herself now. And of others.
She knew how to put these men in their place. A
triumphant smile lit up her face as she looked out the
misty car window.

In less than five minutes, the car turned into one
of the most affluent streets in the city. They stopped
outside giant black gates which had 'Chaudry' written
on them in gaudy golden lettering. One honk and the
gates trembled opened by invisible hands. Velvety red
roses lined the circular driveway as they drove their way
up. The flower pots, stained a garish silver and encrusted
with semi-precious gems, never failed to bring the
expression 'vulgar display of wealth' to her mind, and
now, as they passed cages full of exotic birds and one
that housed a sorry-looking tiger, Radha couldn't help
but feel a rising discomfort. Bubbles were rising in the
pit of her stomach and it was all she could do to stay still
till the car finally stopped at the doorway. Two marble
lions with crystals for eyes sat at the entrance and as
Radha was about to get off, she quelled all her doubts
and turned to the driver. He was staring straight ahead,
as if they had never met.

'You!' she snapped her fingers. 'My name is Radha,
okay? You don't mess with me. Nobody messes
with Radha.'

The boy looked stonily ahead. Satisfied, she slammed the car door behind her.

But, despite the confidence pumping through her veins at this small victory, she felt the usual hesitation as she entered Chaudry Sahib's house. The walls seemed to be laughing at her false bravado, teasing her painted words, taunting her humble beginnings. Or perhaps they were warning her, she thought as goose bumps dimpled her flesh. A sense of foreboding hung in the air, or maybe, Radha consoled herself, it was the scent of expensive tobacco. She forced herself to smile as she took tentative steps forward, a strange force gripping her shoulders, as if pulling her back. She reached a large, carved wooden door, which seemed dark and ominous, much in tune with the heaviness weighing down the air around her. Radha's sheer sari, her glittery nail polish and glossed lips seemed grossly out of place in the melancholy grey of Chaudry Sahib's house. *Like a new bride in a graveyard*, Radha thought, swallowing the lump that had formed in her throat.

She considered turning back, but then she thought of the rain. And of the cheeky driver, whom she had just taught a lesson. *And what of Chaudry Sahib*, she thought. She couldn't afford to lose a client like him. He would be displeased. Very displeased.

'What should I do?' she wondered aloud and, as if on cue, the doors creaked open.

An old man with trembling hands stood to one side to welcome her into the inner wing of the palatial house.

'Radha Bibi, hurry,' he said in a low voice. 'Chaudry Sahib doesn't like to be kept waiting, and you are a whole hour late.'

That alone made her pause, for she knew what these big men could be like when irked.

'The smaller the penis, the bigger the ego,' she mumbled, walking as briskly as her damp sari and wet chappals would allow her to.

Radha knew it was a mistake when she opened the door to the bedroom and saw a half-devoured bottle of whisky on the floor. And two glasses. *Two?* she thought as she looked up to see Chaudry Sahib's face appear slowly from behind the cloud of smoke he was puffing. He put down his cigar, grinding it ruthlessly as if it were a repulsive worm that had slithered unexpectedly on to his person. Seeing her, he got up.

'Oho, welcome jee, welcome, Radha madam,' he said with an exaggerated, theatrical laugh. 'So you finally decided to show up.'

'Sir, woh ... the rain ... I ...' she stammered.

Chaudry waved away her explanation. 'Come, come,' he said.

It's when he moved aside that she saw him. The son. Little currents ran up and down her arms and legs, making her feel numb and dizzy.

'Have you met my son, Nisar, the singer?'

Radha panicked, remembering the stories she had heard on the grapevine and the photos she had seen on WhatsApp, of his face next to an injured girl. *He doesn't look like a killer*, she thought, *but it would've been less disturbing if he hadn't been smiling so menacingly.*

'Aadaab,' she said in a tone that was almost apologetic, for it was all she could do not to turn away and run out the room. The boy had a strange way of smiling so violently that it seemed he wanted to hit the other person.

'You are very late, Radha. I have a meeting with the General Sahib now. But since you are here...I'll leave you with Nisar.'

So *this* was to be her punishment. Radha watched in dismay as Chaudry Sahib sauntered out. This time, there was no one she could call to help.

'Make a man out of him,' her benefactor had demanded as he left the room, leaving her entirely at his mentally disturbed son's mercy. *Make a man?* She had smiled bitterly, thinking, *You can't turn animals into human beings.* But, like a submissive lamb, she had offered herself up. The boy had pawed at her like an animal, a wild animal. Getting more and more drunk with each attack, uncaring, indifferent, his eyes as stony as the whisky glasses reflected in them.

Later, Radha wondered why she hadn't just made a U-turn and run out of the room. But she knew the answer to that well. In the land that they lived in, there was no place to run. All doors were closed on people of her kind. Of her class. Of her gender.

And so she had suffered and swallowed, oohed and ahhed, faking it till the boy finally passed out – a bundle of rupees dangling from his left hand, mocking her. Afterwards, the driver was summoned to take her home. The rain had given way to clear skies and the air was thick with the smell of steaming concrete. There was nothing left of the earlier romance of the monsoons.

Radha clutched miserably at the pallu of her sari, trying to make sense of what had happened to her. She walked stiffly, her hips still sore from where he had entered her despite repeated protests that she didn't provide that kind of service.

'Bitch,' he kept calling her. 'Fucking bitch.'

She looked down at her feet which seemed to be disobeying her every command, dragging when she wanted then to run. Her new chappals no longer seemed new. And she stepped deliberately into a puddle that did little to cleanse her skin. She took one shoe off and threw it hard against the marble lions, not caring if she broke their precious statues, for something much more precious had been shattered today. Her dignity.

As she waited for the car, a torrid wind spitting sand began to rise, unleashing a maelstrom of loose leaves, broken twigs and spiralling plastic bags. The car appeared and, seeing her condition, Abdul Rahim stepped out of the car.

'Madam,' he hesitated.

She got in quietly, eyes downcast. She wondered what he was thinking.

Whatever he thought, the driver kept to himself as he got into the driver's seat and began the slow ride home.

At a signal, he locked eyes with her in the rear-view mirror. But this time his gaze seemed kinder. Gentler.

'Ruqaiyah madam, I take you to hospital?' he enquired.

'No,' she said, alarmed that he could sense what she had suffered. 'Home,' she had pleaded. The earlier bravado replaced by a whisper that just about held back her tears. *Ruqaiyah, Radha ... who cares*, she thought. In the end, she was just a woman. Fashioned out of a rib.

'Take me home,' she repeated weakly.

He didn't argue. He kept driving till, halfway through, when she couldn't help but let the tears seep out of her eyes, he stopped the car. He turned around and stared at her. Just stared as she cried. Then he reached out and took her hand in his.

'Ruqaiyah ji, I will be back.' Saying this, he stepped out.

A few minutes later, he returned with a plastic bag with Dettol and cotton wool.

'May I?' he asked and, like a rag doll, Radha went limp in his arms as he cleaned the tiny cuts around her arms and the scrapes on her skin.

Radha felt one last tear squeeze past her swollen eye.

'Thank you,' she whispered.

'Animals,' the man replied as he held her. 'Animals,' he repeated with even more vigour this time.

Then he shook his head and, to Radha's amazement said, 'No. To call them that is an insult to animals. They are worse. It is about respect, you know. You respect me, I respect you. It's very simple, you know.'

Radha felt a wave of something she told herself must be surprise, for no one had ever stood up for her like this. This man with his kind eyes seemed to know that it wasn't about sex or money, or both. She wasn't a whore. She was a companion, a therapist, a catharsis, for she listened, she pleasured, she pleased. And perhaps that's why Chaudry Sahib had entrusted his son to her.

She opened her swollen mouth to say something, but the pain was unbearable. So she stayed quiet, alternating between gazing into the driver's kind eyes and at her fancy chappals.

When they reached her house, the driver once again glanced at her and said, 'You are very strong, madam. And beautiful.'

A warmth enveloped her and she told him to wait. She would pay him for the medicines.

'Ek minute,' she said, as she slowly got out of the car and went inside.

'Arrey no, no,' he protested, but she insisted.

Once inside, she took out a couple of hundred-rupee notes and called to her maid. The lights flickered as the rain began again, and she realized with a start that she had let Shanti go almost a month ago. Clutching the notes and pouring out a glass of water, she walked with a slight limp towards the door she had left ajar.

She was about to call him in when she heard him speaking. He seemed to be talking on the phone and laughing at something. Radha too felt her lips stretch painfully in a smile. She was about to step out when she heard his voice again.

'No, no. VIP passenger, yaar. Just dropping off an old whore who got beaten up.'

Radha froze, hand on the doorknob, foot raised mid-step.

'Calls herself *Radha*.' She heard him laugh again. 'Thinks she's a sixteen-year-old Alia Bhatt. Chal, rakhta hoon.'

Outside, the driver had turned on the radio and was humming a tune.

'Radha likes to party, Radha likes to move...'

Radha felt her face streaming wet and wondered how it was that it was raining inside.

She forced herself to step out, hoping the rain would disguise her tears as she handed him the money.

'There was no need,' he said as he pocketed the money.'

'It's your tip,' she said, watching as the boy's expression hardened.

'Thank you, Ruqaiyah ji.'

'Radha,' she said, looking firmly into his eyes. 'My name is Radha.'

And with that she limped slowly back inside, shutting the door firmly behind her.

An Irreplaceable Loss

The girl felt as if she would explode. Nevertheless, she kept a straight face as the agent negotiated her pay with the new baji.

'24/7 rates, Baji. I am not just giving you a new maid, I am giving you my daughter. At least pay a few thousand more.'

The girl inhaled deeply, trying hard to stifle her laughter. She was neither young enough to be his daughter, nor he mature enough to act like someone's father. It was all she could do to hold back her laughter, for her sudden, uncontrollable fits of giggles had already cost her the last job where she had laughed at the baji's new haircut, or the one before that when she had laughed at the fat kid whose mother couldn't stop telling people how her son never ate anything. She sucked in her already sunken stomach and forced herself to think of the time she had cut her foot on a piece of sharp glass.

'Baji ji, she is very hard worker,' the agent was saying. 'Only sixteen, but works like a horse.'

The baji looked her up and down but didn't say anything.

'Don't go by her young looks. Believe me, she is very strong.'

The baji looked sceptical but remained silent.

The silent type, the girl thought. Those were the toughest. No words. Slaps and kicks straightaway. Sometimes burns. She didn't feel like laughing so much now.

Tough, tougher, toughest.

Later, once the agent left her alone there, having taken half her salary in advance as his fee, the baji finally turned to her.

'How old are you, really?'

The girl tried hard to remember what the agent had told her.

'Fifteen,' she said, scratching her head. 'No, Baji. Sixteen!'

The woman rolled her eyes and asked, 'What did you do at the last house?'

'Dusting, sweeping, laundry.'

'Why did you leave it?'

The girl shuffled a little and replied, 'My old baji moved to Dubai.'

The woman in the chair threw back her head and laughed. 'You all have the same excuse. At this rate, there would be no women left in all of Pakistan to hire you people.'

The girl watched in fascination the baji's pearly teeth and her melodious laughter, making a mental note to practise it quietly at night.

When the woman stopped laughing, she asked, 'What's your name?'

'Tarannum,' the girl replied.

'Real name,' the baji said, tapping her foot impatiently.

'Baji, that is my real name.'

She could tell the baji didn't believe her, for her name meant 'melody', hardly a name someone would give to the fifth daughter of a drug addict and a malnutritioned mother who cleaned houses.

'You can ask the agent,' the girl offered, seeing the suspicious look in the eyes of her new mistress, for surely her kind didn't think poor people could have the imagination to name their children so creatively. Anyhow, she consoled herself, she was used to this. None of the three houses she had worked at before had called her by her real name, finding it either too fake or too filmy.

'Call him, Baji. You can check. I'm not lying...'

'No need,' the woman waved a manicured hand with glossy pink nails at her. 'Look, I'll just call you ...' the baji paused to think, and the girl admired the way her lashes seemed to roll back, the clumpy mascara only adding to the thickness.

She smiled, slightly excited at the prospect of getting yet another new name. And sure enough, she did not have to wait too long.

'I will call you Tooba. Tarannum sounds too ...' the baji's voice trailed off, but her silence had said more than her words ever could.

Doesn't sound like a maid's name, the girl completed the woman's sentence in her heart.

Just then, the woman's cellphone rang and the girl watched as she picked it up with her delicate, fair hands, and started speaking in English. The girl loved the sound of English and observed closely, picking up familiar words here and there, tucking them into her memory, the way she collected shells at the dirty, garbage-filled beach her Abba took her to on Sundays, hoping to string them in a necklace someday.

'Okay ...' the baji said, clicking off her phone and turning to where the girl sat on the floor. She looked distracted for a second, trying to remember the name she had given the new maid.

'Tooba,' the girl supplied helpfully.

'Yeah, yeah,' the woman said. 'Saima,' she bellowed, and a stocky, middle-aged woman appeared almost instantly. 'Now listen, Tooba. Saima here is my oldest maid. She will show you the work around the house. You can share her quarters. Now look, I didn't argue about the salary, so you must not give me a reason to cut any. No going outside without my permission; no talking to the cook or driver. I want you to take a bath every other day. There is a water problem, so don't get carried away, okay? One bucket per bath for all servants. And most importantly, trust. My things ... any of my things ... better not go missing. Understand? Okay, now go.'

The girl got up, thinking, same rules everywhere. She wondered if there was a baji rule book they all followed religiously. She placed her hands on the cold floor to raise herself and was about to follow the tough-looking Saima, when the baji called her back.

'Tooba,' she said, and at first the girl, unused to the new name, continued to walk.

'Girl, are you deaf?' the older maid nudged her.

'Hah?' The girl turned around to see the baji looking irritably at her as she ran her fingers through her long, expensive-looking hair.

'I almost forgot,' the baji said, looking sternly at her as if it were her fault, 'Hand over your cellphone.'

The girl looked at her toes. Hard and stubby with chipped red polish that looked more angry than stylish.

'Well?'

She looked back up to the baji's hand, outstretched and impatient. 'Hurry up,' she said.

The girl continued to look down.

'Listen, I will give it to you if you need to call home.'

'Baji,' she began, 'I ... I...'

The woman leaned forward in her chair. 'Look, I don't allow any affairs-shaffairs, okay? Now hand over the phone and go.'

'I don't have one,' the girl said without looking up.

The woman stared at her in silence for a good few seconds before she spoke.

'Listen, if I find one on you, I'll fire you without pay!' The baji's face took on a hard, impenetrable quality and for a moment the girl considered surrendering it. But then she thought, *What if* he *calls?*

She looked down again, this time at the patterns on the plush Persian carpet, and nodded mutely.

'Okay then, go.'

Going, going, gone.

The first thing the girl did as soon as they left the baji's room was to ask for the toilet. There, she squatted down on the floor, putting her phone on silent, and rolled it into the waistband of her shalwar. She wondered if he would call. Their eyes had met, however briefly, in the car ride here, and she had made sure she gave her number out loud to the agent before stepping out of the car.

The baji had sent her driver to pick them up when the maid provider couldn't find the address. And in the car, he had locked eyes with her in the rear-view mirror, of that she was sure. She chewed her chadder, partly covering her face, but when she got off the car, she had turned around to look. He was looking straight at her. It had meant something, she told herself. It had to.

Phone safely hidden, she emerged from the bathroom, head covered, eyes down, and got to work, which was the same in all Karachi houses.

Dust, dusty, dustier.

She worked while her mind dreamt. And she mostly got away with it, for there were many servants in the house and Baji didn't run a tight ship. Every now and then, she would flare up, making everyone run around cleaning the big house; but in the next few days, she would forget all about it. Only a few times, she had been cleaning the baji's room or massaging her legs when her phone had started vibrating and she had shifted uncomfortably from leg to leg, wanting to sink into the ground, hoping against hope that she would not notice.

Shift, shifty, shiftiest.

It took barely a few days for him to text her. And not surprising, for she had seen him stare at her when she went out to the terrace to dry the laundry.

'I love u,' the message read, and she felt a warmth surge up between her thighs. That night, she ducked into the bathroom and locked the door. She ignored the knocking on the door, feigning diarrhoea, as she texted back, 'I love u 2.'

He rang back.

After ten minutes of hurried whispering, the phone began to beep 'credit finished'.

The few minutes of talking did nothing for either of them, and so it was that after a few nights, the girl agreed to meet him.

'About 3.00 a.m., I'll call you when I'm outside the front door,' the man had said.

The girl had not thought much about what she was about to do, for she didn't have much to lose. Her possessions were few and her dignity was stripped every day by taunts and accusations of work not done. Hell, even her name was not her own.

And so it was she told the man: 'I'll open the front door and you slip in. That old maid Saima sleeps like a drunk. The baji stays up late watching TV, but she sits with the air-conditioner on, which drowns out all noise.'

Come, coming, came.

And that was how the girl lost her latest job and her latest name too, when one night, possessed by one of her sudden cleaning frenzies, the baji summoned all her staff in the middle of the night. Having come across an unexpected cobweb as she reached for a DVD in the wrought-iron rack, she squawked in terror when, instead of a disc, her hand pulled out a spider.

'Saima! Tooba!' the baji screamed as if her very self was under attack. 'Cook! Houseboy!' All the servants came running. Only, Tooba could not be found. A thorough inspection led to the girl being found on the formal dining table, under the driver. The cellphone lay guiltily next to them.

Phone, phony, phonier.

The perils of a big city are also its plus points. Both the girl and the driver found new jobs with new names shortly thereafter. However, they say, the baji has still not gotten over the loss. She could no longer bear to eat at the table, knowing what had been served on it. The grief of replacing the table had caused her much agony, for as she was often heard saying, 'Good dining tables are so hard to find.' Her soft brown eyes would fill with tears at this, causing her coloured contacts to itch. Another thing that she found so hard to bear about life in Karachi – amidst the dust, the breaking of trust and, of course, the loss of valuables.

'Why is life so hard?' the woman was often heard saying.

Hard, harder, hardly.

The Adulteress

She thought of him as she folded the clothes. She thought of him as she put them away. She thought of him as she walked on autopilot to the kitchen. She thought of him as she opened the fridge and pulled out the okra. Without washing the vegetables, she began to chop mechanically, the sharp green needle-like tips reminding her of his beak-shaped nose.

That was today.

Halfway through the chopping, she put down the knife. She seemed to be straining to hear something. Abruptly, she got up and walked towards the open door of the balcony.

'Purday mein rehne do, purdah na uthao...'

The words from an old film song drifted up towards her. And she inhaled them slowly, as if they were the aroma of a rich home brew. She found her heart slowing down. Her palms felt cold and she had to lean against the metal railings to steady herself. She remembered watching the film with her parents when she was a little girl. VCRs were a new thing in those days, obsolete as they are now. And she smiled at the thought of trying to explain to her children what they were. For a moment, and just a moment, the thought distracted her.

The shrill ringing of the phone broke into her thoughts and she looked guiltily at her mobile writhing on the table. For some inexplicable reason, its vibration reminded her of the dancers in the films of that era. 'Helen,' she whispered softly, smiling and shaking her head at the memory of the cabaret dancer, jerking her body in impossibly swift movements at breakneck speed. Everything was so black-and-white in those days, she thought. The roles of the good girl and the bad girl clearly defined. The heroine and the vamp, never mixed. *That was then.*

The phone stopped ringing and the stillness of the silence pressed upon her now. The radio downstairs had been switched off and she heard the banging of a door, as if someone had left the house. She was alone now. Alone with her thoughts. A tangible panic gripped her throat, as if trying to trap her. A thousand fingers clutching her neck and jaw. The sun seemed brighter, the wind harsher. She closed her eyes and a face appeared behind the closed lids. It doubled into faces. Faces which were looking at her with great trust. You are not Helen, they assured her. And she opened her eyes and started to laugh. But the laughter provided little relief. The restlessness within her was growing with as much thrust and power as that of a magical beanstalk. She wanted to do something, but what? As if to curb some mysterious urge, she pushed a flowerpot off the balcony's edge. Immediately, she took a step back, waiting for the sound of a crash. She waited for a loud thud, perhaps a scream, a yelp, a reproach. When none came, she leaned forward and saw that the plant had fallen on the clean white sheets of her ground-floor neighbour, which she had hung out to dry. The now-soiled sheets had cushioned the fall and fluttered up at her as if to say a half-hearted hello. She stepped back again, placing a hand on her forehead as if to check her own temperature. This was unlike her. Since when had she become so destructive? And with a deep frown, she wondered, so wasteful?

This was now.

She waited for her neighbour to shout, but no sound travelled up and she exhaled – slowly, deeply. It was a slippery feeling, she thought, the relief of getting away with something. She looked up at the white-hot sun which looked like a hole burned in a blue cloth by some careless god, and touched her throat. Her neck. Finally, her fingers rested on the space between her breasts. She pressed the hard bit. The bone or the cage or whatever it was that kept her heart from escaping. Assured by the beating drums inside her, she allowed herself to think back. *To him.* It came to her in little flashes, like swatches of colour, like sudden sparks from dying embers. The memory of being with another man was something her mind seemed to block and obsess over at the same time. For a moment, she was reminded of the coloured-chalk drawings she would draw on the sidewalk when she was a little girl and how each morning the sweeper would come and wash them away with a bucket of water. What surprised her was how nothing had changed. Her daily routine, her children's demands, her husband's indifference... Everything around her remained the same.

Except her.

She turned away. Away from the light and the wide open sky before her, and headed back to her dark, airless kitchen. It was a space she knew well.

In the familiar arena of her domain, she inhaled the scents of peeled garlic, the nauseating stench of chopped onions and the suffocating smell of raw ginger. She allowed herself to wonder, if only for a second, how it had happened.

Neither had expected it to happen. She a mother of three and he a divorcee rebuilding the foundations of his life, cherishing his new-found freedom, wearing his heart on his sleeve. Perhaps that is what they both had in common, these two completely unlikely beings. A few moments of escape. Neither felt they were ready to let go of this precious free-floating state they found themselves in. Perhaps they wanted to hold on, just a little bit longer.

Now back in the kitchen as she chopped the okra, she felt certain that it was the man who had made the first move. She put the knife aside for a second and leaned back against the counter. Had she given him any sign at all? No, she decided. She hadn't even imagined the possibility. Never thought of herself as someone who cheated. But could this be called infidelity?

'Infidelity,' she tried out the word on her tongue. 'Infidel,' she said, looking guiltily out of the door towards the Arabic verses embroidered into the wall hanging. Was she an infidel, she wondered, pulling her dupatta close to her skin. But try as she might, she couldn't feel the guilt. Instead, all she felt was a strange kind of bewilderment. Surprised that something so extraordinary could happen to someone as ordinary as her. All she knew was that night, she had felt like a jug being emptied, a vessel that had poured out everything that was inside. But afterwards, she didn't feel hollowed out. Instead, she felt fulfilled. Content. As if she had gained something. Or perhaps ... she frowned, perhaps it was the weight of the secret she carried within her body. For a second she wondered what would happen if her husband or her children found out. She traced the outline of the garlic on her chopping board. Adulteress, she wrote, arranging the pods in a trail of letters ... Adultery, adult, idol, idolatry, adulatory...

Except there was no betrayal. She had made it all up. Yes, she nodded. It was best to think this a product of her imagination. To pen it down and preserve it in her memory forever as fiction.

A cry escaped her lips as she realized she had cut herself with the knife's edge. A strange feeling of foreboding washed over her – a shudder, as if she had seen death's angel. She felt herself shiver violently as a fat drop of blood landed on the cutting board, its scarlet hue disappearing into the wood almost immediately. A few seconds later, it was as if it had never happened.

Her skin, she noticed, was already beginning to heal.

It was then she realized that it didn't matter what stories they told other people, it was the stories we tell our own selves that mattered. Addressing the limp okra that lay split open like ancient soldiers defeated on a battlefield, she said, 'We are all made up of stories. The stories we tell others, the stories we tell ourselves and, most importantly, the stories we hide. Deep inside.'

Cocking her head to one side, she waited for the lifeless vegetables to respond. It occurred to her that there was a reason why invalids were addressed as vegetables. Enough, she said to herself as she willed her thoughts to focus. Her husband was a good man, she told herself, as she went back to the 'thak thak' of the chopping board, bashing the garlic this time. She lifted one pale crescent and held it close to her nose. The strong odour wafted to her nostrils and she thought back to the other man's scent. She had sniffed his armpits like a dog. Like a small bitch sniffing her master, trying to memorize his smell. Encapsulate it. Perhaps to enhance her senses when once again the monotony of life got too much.

A wave of nausea washed over her. *How could she?* Her jaw tightened and she felt her limbs stiffen. *Why shouldn't she?*

Now, as she chopped the onions – always the last, as they made her cry – she let the anger flow through her. The rage when it had come had surprised her, for she was a gentle woman. Not easily irked, though there was much that moved her. She'd always cherished that delusional quality of hers, for she lived life as if it were some dream sequence. Nothing mattered much in her scheme of things. A beautiful jewel that she couldn't have, a perfect home, or even the love she expected from her husband ... long ago, she had learnt not to expect. For expectations were like promises – made to be broken. Early in her marriage, she had learnt that beauty was a thing to be cherished and love was fleeting. Her highs were her emotions, but there were no great storms in her teacup to stir them. She led a mundane life. An ordinary housewife married to an ordinary man. A life of rationing, measuring, saving and counting. But like the heroines of the books she had read, like Emma Bovary and Anna Karenina, she longed to escape that mundane life. And so she had taken to writing.

And it was her words that had provided her an escape. Not just metaphorically but physically too. She wrote many stories. Mostly love stories about stormy romances between fiery heroines and gentle heroes. Stories through which she lived her life. Sometimes she would show them to her friends, who encouraged her to submit them to women's magazines. One day, a cheque arrived for her along with an acceptance. Holding that little piece of paper in her hand gave her more joy than the birth of all three of her children.

Soon she began writing with a seriousness she did not know she was capable of. In the morning, as soon as she had sent off her husband and children and finished the morning chores, she would sit down in the balcony and begin to write. Words came naturally to her. She could take a thought and make it come alive, her friends would tell her. And as she honed her craft, she became stronger emotionally too. Soon, she was publishing two to three stories a month and getting a steady, if small, income that made her feel more powerful than she had ever felt in her life. At first, she kept it from her husband; but as her fame began to grow, she showed him the magazines with her name inside. She remembered how he had patted her head, as if indulging her. She remembered that indignant feeling that had overcome her whole body. His reaction was similar to her presenting him with a new recipe, his patronizing expression the same as when she stood back in anticipation while he raised a spoonful to his lips.

She wondered now if it was this exasperation that made her do what she did.

Adding the oil into the pan, she watched as hot drops hissed at her. Something was bubbling inside her too. Was it anger, resentment or just regret? Perhaps all three, she thought as she recalled with wonder how she had let him enter the boundaries she had so carefully built around herself. He had entered unopposed.

First her body. And later, her mind.

The man had called her out of the blue. He introduced himself first as an admirer of her work and then as a journalist, and much later as a poet. They were launching a women's magazine. Would she attend the opening ceremony? The first thoughts that had run through her mind – like a ticker at the bottom of a news channel – were, who would mind the kids, what would her husband say, how would she get there, how would she find her way to the venue … And then in a moment which surprised even her, she heard her voice say 'yes'.

'Wonderful,' the man had said, 'we'll send a car for you.' And so she had found herself giving out her address to him.

And on the day, everything had worked like clockwork. Her neighbour had offered to look after the children, her husband had said he was working late. No explanations were needed, none given.

And so the opening night of the magazine became her opening night too, for she felt she was exploring a world of possibilities. Outside her home, she was not just a mother or a wife, but a writer. A person of her own.

And why shouldn't she be?

He was a poet by passion and a journalist by profession. He told her that he liked her craft. And that he liked her even more. Perhaps he didn't even say that. Perhaps she had made it all up...

She was no longer sure what she had heard or what he had said. All she remembered was that she had listened to him talk and, when it was time to go, he offered to drop her back. On the way home, he had leaned towards her. She was not sure why she allowed it, but she did. On that secluded Karachi street, under the veil of darkness, she let down a closely guarded boundary, till a sudden flash of headlights made her realize she was not in one of her stories but in a stranger's car, with a strange man who was not her husband.

The thought thrilled her even more.

Now back in her small, airless kitchen, she turned away from the stove and poured herself a glass of cold water. The chilling sensation as the water made its way down her throat made her pause. She wanted to remember it.

Like a prisoner who doesn't let go of the pain, she too wanted to hold on. It reminded her of her enslavement. For she made sure she never saw him again.

But that didn't stop her thinking about him.

She held the glass to her lips, pressed hard against the flesh, then on an impulse threw the remaining water into the pan. Steam rose and she thought to herself, fire takes time to cool down.

Had it really been a year?

He had kissed her softly at first, like a lamb grazing a field. Then, sensing no resistance, hungrily, almost savagely. So harshly that she felt consumed by him. She felt the weight of his body as he leaned into her, its heaviness as alarming as it was exciting. Pressed under his warm body, she was surprised to find that she did not feel suffocated. Instead she felt as if she had been drifting and finally her hands had grabbed an anchor. It was unlike any other feeling she had imagined. And it was only when the sadness began to lift that she realized she had been sad. So very sad. Unfeeling, numb and blank. Like one of her pages. Before she decorated them with words, projecting her feelings on the pages, blending her emotions into a barrage of stories. Exchanging loneliness for imagination. Concealing, erasing, hiding, behind words.

And then a sudden flash of light had erased it all. She had felt as if she had been found out. When the headlights of a passing car had flashed upon them, the man had his hand on her breast. The word 'trespass' sounded in her head like an alarm. A sudden revulsion filled her at the sight of this stranger who only a moment ago had excited her. His praise of her writing talent had made her shiver with pleasure. He had made her feel genuine, worthy, as if she mattered. As if her only role in life was not to be just a wife or a mother. Her calling in life was not just to serve others.

Or to be served.

But when the harsh light lit up his face, she realized that once again she was being used. In that moment, it didn't matter what face the man took on. She was just a feast he was preparing to swallow. A rage surged through her. She wasn't ready for this. She wasn't up for grabs. And in the passing glare of the lights, she felt cheap. She shook her head. She told him to stop.

What took her by surprise was that he stopped. No one had ever really listened to what she wanted. Perhaps that was why she spoke through her characters. And now, as she felt the power of her own voice, through some strange intuitiveness, she felt as if this man, trying to calm her down and assuring her that he would not touch her unless she wanted him to, was listening.

Something inside her shifted. *She had been heard.* And in that moment, she had understood that her life was hers to live. Her voice was hers to use. And for that, she was grateful to him.

But would she ever have the courage to be herself again? To raise her voice, to say aloud what she was thinking, to express what she felt, to do what she really wanted?

She realized then that it wasn't her husband she had been unfaithful to. The real betrayal was to herself. It was her own true self that she had been cheating. She knew that she was more than what her home life allowed her to be. She knew she had talent. She could be someone. But she could not even admit this to herself. Every time she tried to introduce herself as a writer, she felt like an imposter. Yet as a wife and a mother, too, she felt as if she was playing a part. What then was her true self?

'Ding dong! Ding dong!' The incessant chiming of the doorbell made her look around with the surprised daze of someone who had just woken up from a deep slumber.

'Coming,' she shouted. A violent sneeze shook her as she realized that much more time had passed than she had anticipated.

'Thak, thak!' Multiple fists knocked at the door.

A quick glance at the wall clock told her that the children were back home.

'Ammi, open the door,' their voices echoed from outside.

'The children,' she sighed, as she wiped her hands on her dupatta. Smoke itched her nose and stung her eyes. Just as she was about to leave the kitchen, her glance fell on the stove. She stopped even as their voices outside rose and dropped like the waves in an ocean. She stared in wonder, for an acrid smoke rose from the pan. The okra was charred. Black. She removed the pan from the stove, only to realize a low flame was still on.

Strangely, she could not remember lighting it.

The Lovers

It was the time of the year when day merges into night without a single change of light. We lay on our stomachs on the grass, our legs criss-crossing behind us like a pair of scissors, our mouths stuffed with illicit chocolates. It was 1986. The city was London and I was seven. Everything was as it ought to have been.

Next to me lay my cousin Ready. He had a habit of spreading his nine-year-old body like a dead crab and being absolutely still, at times, not even blinking.

'Ready!' I said. Not a single movement. I wondered again why he was called Ready, for he was anything but. No matter what the occasion. The only thing he could do was eat. And when he wasn't eating, he was hiding. And when he was hiding, it was usually because he was eating.

First published in *Bengal Lights*, 2013.

He'd been eating a doughnut the first time I saw him. We'd arrived from a small town just outside of Lahore to their semi-detached house in a sprawling suburban London council estate. My father hoped to find a job nearby and till then we were to stay with relatives we had never met before. Four people stood in a row at the doorway in descending order of height. At first, they seemed to me like any other Pakistani-English family. Ready's father, especially, was a cut-to-cut copy of my own. Tall, imposing and silent. His mother, however, seemed a little different from mine. I couldn't pinpoint it, but later at dinner, when her scarf kept sliding off her head, I realized it was because she probably didn't wear it all the time like my mother. Mummy Jee however quickly got out a heap of hairpins and nailed it in place. For the rest of our stay, it stayed glued to Aunty's head, as if it had been painted on.

And then there was Aliya, Ready's older sister and fifteen.

'*That* age', my mother had said. When I asked what she meant, Mummy Jee gave me a look and told me off for eavesdropping.

'How could it be eavesdropping if you are talking right in front of us?' I argued, but she did not answer. She did that a lot. When I exceeded the number of questions I was allowed to ask, which was usually no more than two, she told me to go play.

'But play what?' I would ask, and be met with silence.

And so today, here I was, lolling on the grass with Ready after being told to go play, which Ready explained actually meant 'go away' when said by adults. But now that we saw Aliya approaching, it meant we had been summoned back and whatever it was that had been brewing between our mothers was over. Since our arrival, at least one hour a day was spent with Mummy Jee lecturing Aunty about something or the other that needed correcting. Today, they had been gesturing wildly with their hands, shaking their heads as their voices rose between shrill highs and almost whispers. In between, my mother cursed the Whites and the Blacks and someone else whose true colours, she said, were yet to be seen.

Unlike Ready, Aliya was tall and thin, with a long black ponytail tumbling down her back. I thought it made her look like a mermaid. And perhaps for this reason, her mother had told her this morning to put on a headscarf. Standing behind her, Mummy Jee looked like an extra head that had grown over Aunty's shoulder as she nodded approvingly and threw in a few words of her own for good measure.

'Never trust the stranger's gaze,' she warned Aliya. 'Men in this country have only one thing on their minds. God forbid, even the women here you can't trust!'

Aliya listened patiently, then left the house slamming the door behind her. She came home just before her father was due back and, amidst much shouting and tears, Aunty threatened to tell him if she ever did that again. My mother took her place over the shoulder and said, 'What would the relatives in Pakistan say!'

Once again, Aliya listened wordlessly, then went up to her room. The sound of furious typing could be heard as she jabbed the keys of the old typewriter that took up most of her desk.

'Ya Allah,' my mother exclaimed. 'What on earth is that noise? It sounds like a machine gun.'

Aunty smiled and said, 'No, no, sister, my Aliya likes to write. She even got a prize for a poem.'

'Do you know what we call women who write poetry in our culture?' Mummy Jee snickered, 'Courtesans!'

'No, no,' Aunty said. 'It is for schoolwork...'

Mummy Jee placed her hand on Aunty's arm and smiled her most patient smile. 'Ishrat, you are so naive. All this poetry-shoetry is not good for our girls. Puts all kinds of ideas in their heads. Romance-shomance...'

'But, sister,' Aunty said, 'it's part of her schoolwork. And my daughter must study. Just think, if she is educated, at least she will have some choice in life. You know my neighbour is a sixty-year-old woman who lives by herself! I tell you...'

Mother pressed a palm over her mouth. 'It is all this London-Shondon's doing. Back home, nobody would even *think* such a thing. You will see, Ishrat. You will see the result of all your mod-run talk when your daughter runs off with a foreigner!'

While Mummy Jee berated Aunty, Ready and I took advantage of the situation and asked to go to the sweet shop. They nodded distractedly.

'Money?' I asked.

Not wanting to let go of this opportunity, Mummy untied the end of her dupatta and thrust a pound coin in my hand.

'Lay phur,' she said, 'now go play.'

That was our cue to race out of the house and towards the corner shop at the end of the street. Though it was still bright, I knew it was late in the day. It felt good to be out in London, at what – going by the clock, at least – was night time. Ready and I entered the shop full of excitement, but before we could reach the pic 'n' mix section, we stopped dead in our tracks.

Aliya stood before us, tall and lanky in her jeans, her headscarf lopsided as if it had dropped unexpectedly on her head. She looked equally shocked, by the look of her half-open mouth. Quickly, she slipped her hand in her pocket and it was then I noticed what she had been holding. Another hand.

Like the Churchill dog I had seen in the insurance advert, our heads bobbed up and down as we traced the hand that now hung limp by the side of the person, to his face. A brown face. We felt our shoulders drop and our necks relax, but then Aliya said, 'This is my friend, Ram.'

If I could pin one moment in my life when I instinctively knew my right from wrong without anyone telling me so, it was this. I knew intuitively that I should not be where I was, had not meant to see what I saw and was not prepared to hear what I was hearing. I looked at Ready and nodded. It was time to do what my cousin did best: disappear.

Later, under the makeshift tent in his bedroom, we felt the bedsheet rise. Aliya peered in at us, her jet-black pupils dilating, then suddenly enlarging as she leaned in towards us. She said nothing and we pretended to ignore her. But after the sheet dropped back down, both of us let out a long, slow breath.

'Ready?' Ready asked, and we both snuck as far back under the tent as we possibly could without popping out from the other side.

As it so often happens in life when we want to bury something deep down inside ourselves, our bodies try to throw it back up. First, Ready and I had a bout of vomiting. This was followed by a persistent cough. As we coughed and sneezed, it was all we could do to keep the words slipping out with the phlegm. When that settled, we developed a constant itch. As we scratched our skins, our tongues itched to unload the secret our hearts refused to bury.

We avoided the grown-ups to the point that, one day, just before we were to leave for Bradford where my father had found a job, my mother caught me by the ear and said, 'Out with it! What have you broken, you little devil, and where have you hidden it?'

A string of wasn't-mes followed, but she would have none of it. 'Hand it over,' she said, pointing to the revered candies. I reached into my pocket, but as my hand drew out the toffees, the words slipped out too. 'We saw Aliya with a boy.' Instantly, my body felt lighter.

My mother's eyes widened and I watched her forehead disappear under her headscarf. 'I *knew* it,' she said, and the load shifted to my heart. It felt heavy and slippery as it sank lower and lower into the cavity of my chest, stopping just before it dropped into my stomach.

'Please don't hurt her.'

'Go play.'

'But,' I protested.

'Just leave, and don't say a word to anyone.'

Shutting the door behind me, I saw Mummy Jee take Aunty's elbow and turn her around.

In the evening, before we left their house, Aliya gave me a chocolate bar.

'Thank you,' she whispered and I nodded, feeling guilty for letting her think her secret was safe with me. Try as I might, I could not eat her offering. I left London holding on to the now sticky, sweaty chocolate, waving a sluggish goodbye to my new friends. I wondered when I would see them again.

As it happens, I didn't have to wait too long. During the Christmas break, my father had to go to London for work and, following Mummy Jee's relentless grumbling about it being a woman's fate to be left behind while the men went out to enjoy, he took us along. This time, we went to Ready's house only for lunch.

The first thing I noticed was how bare it seemed. The house was strangely quiet – not just in sound but in appearance too. After a while, I noticed all the pictures were gone. Even the family photographs had been removed. Just then, Ready came down. I was surprised to see him. He had lost weight and, when he opened his mouth, only a squeak emerged.

My mother shook her head and smiled. 'You are very nearly a man now,' she said. He turned a deep shade of red before disappearing just as quietly as he had appeared.

Later at lunch, I asked Ready if he wanted to play, but he turned away.

'Men,' my mother said and laughed.

'Where is Aliya?' I asked as Aunty served us. 'Is she busy with her poetry?' I giggled, winking at Ready as I did so. When he flinched, I looked up at Aunty who looked up at Uncle who looked away.

'We sent her to Pakistan,' he said.

A silence descended upon the room, with the only sound punctuating the air being that of my mother's chewing and swallowing.

'Very good thing you did,' my mother said, tucking a few stray strands of hair back under Aunty's headscarf. Mummy's hands flew busily above Aunty's head like a pair of pesky flies as she pulled pins from her own head and tucked them into Aunty's. 'Who knows what shame-vame she would have brought to the family's honour?' A thin glint of saliva gleamed at the corners of her mouth.

Before we left, I asked Aunty if I could go up to Aliya's room. Inside, her old typewriter sat silent, its keys like hollowed dead eyes, its clownish smile reminding me of that first journey to London. I took a chocolate from my pocket and placed it under its rusty keys. Her old headscarf lay discarded at the edge, as if she had just gone out for a walk and would come back any time. I picked it up.

Before leaving, I covered the typewriter with her hijab.

A World without Men

In ordinary circumstances, I would have taken her in. But this was an extraordinary situation. Firstly, she was my student. Secondly, she was a Muslim. Thirdly, she was invisible.

Complicated as it sounds, it wasn't really. The invisibility had more to do with being shrouded from head to toe in an elaborate veil than with anything more technical. And believe you me, the jilbab, as she called the all-encompassing veil, was the least of our complications. I suppose having something of a relationship with your student was higher on the list of risks. Albeit not as high as when the student is from an orthodox Muslim family with borderline bipolar tendencies and you are not:

a) a Muslim
b) a man
c) a lesbian.

Well, enough with the guessing game. I must let the story tell itself. Funny that I call it a story, for when I first started writing, I never thought I would be mining my own life for material. But there you have it, a classic case of 'write what you know'.

It all began simply enough. Not a very exciting beginning, I know, but bear with me, for the simplicity is deceptive. And that's what my life has been all along – a paradox, an oxymoron, or in layman terms, something that looks simple on the surface but has so many tangled roots beneath it that my tongue grows fuzzy at the thought of an analogy that even begins to describe the mess my life is. Which is ironic, because only a few months ago, there would have been a deluge of literary terms ready to rush out of my big mouth. Why? Well, because that's what I did for a living. Lecture. And that too, on the art of creativity.

I grew up outside London and had a relatively normal childhood with a set of parents, unlike most other children in my neighbourhood who were brought up by single mothers. I was a happy child, fair-haired, with a ready smile, who grew up a confident young woman. That is, until I had my accident. Too much drinking and some other distractions led to me stepping in front of a bus late one night. I survived, but my self-esteem didn't. A nasty gash on my forehead and a slight limp left me needy and confused. A point came when I felt the need to tell my story. I had a college degree in Humanities, but the desire to write had overcome everything. One failed novel later, I turned to teaching other aspiring writers how *not* to write.

Increasingly, I was beginning to realize that everyone had a book inside them and, just as a difficult labour can be eased with Epidural, they too needed help giving birth to the written word. Stillborns, or alive and kicking, was not up to me. My job was to help deliver. And so, instead of teaching the dead white writers whom no one wanted to read any more, I began teaching creative writing. The Art of Creativity is what my course was called, and I loved teaching it – or I used to, till I moved to this godforsaken town.

Strange how life takes unexpected turns. A year ago, I'd been living in London, happily married, with a secure job, an antique aga in my kitchen and a cat (a proper Persian one at that). And then the recession hit. Utility took over creativity and business began to suffer. At the same time, my husband got a redundancy package and, instead of wallowing in self-pity like most men would do, he decided he wanted to travel the world – alone. He argued he wanted to rediscover himself and, like a graceful loser, I gave in. But, as they say, bad luck comes in threes. The cat ran away and the aga got a gas leak. To cut a long story short, my life fell apart.

And I would have stayed under the covers, my head buried deep like an ostrich, if the husband hadn't demanded we rent out the house. 'It's too big for one person. And you are not earning enough to pay the mortgage,' he argued. 'We're going to end up losing the house,' he said with the conviction of a clairvoyant, making me truly doubt my ability to manage my life. 'Your stubbornness will go swimming in the sea if we miss any more mortgage payments,' he went on. *Always the logical one*, I thought, yielding to his will.

The husband and I parted ways, promising to meet in six months' time to review our feelings. The money was bound to run out by then, I consoled myself, and he would return with his tail tucked between his legs. I told myself it would all work out in the end. It always did. I should have known then that there was something wrong with me.

And so it was that I found myself thrown out of my own house as we let it to complete strangers for six months. Since it was a short let, we left all our things in the house. I still remember the strange feeling of being suspended in mid-air as I handed over my keys. I imagined the tenants lying down on my bed, sleeping on my pillow, using my toilet seat, and I felt like throwing up. The next few days, I stayed with a friend who constantly berated me for giving in to my conniving husband's machinations. 'How could you be so naïve?' she said, throwing up her hands in the air. 'How could you let him kick you out of the house, out of his life ...' After three days of her incessant nagging, I left without leaving a note.

The whole episode made me want to get as far away from London as possible (while remaining on a train route, just in case I had to come back in a hurry). I scoured the job ads and found a few positions worth applying for up north. I still don't know what it was that attracted me to that godforsaken town, but then again, if we could explain our choices rationally, what drama would there be in life? And so it was that without any logic or reason, I moved to Leicester and found myself teaching the same Dead White Male writers I had come to abhor.

Leicester was painful. And not just visually. The people looked like the ones I had spent a lifetime trying to get away from by moving to London. Suburban. Not a shred of urbanism in this place masquerading as a city. I shuddered to think that I might slip into their sloppiness and promised myself to stay away from puffy parkas, black trousers and imitation leather. But it didn't matter how I dressed. I could never fit into their world. The students always laughed at me. In retrospect, I think they laughed at all the teachers. But at that time, struggling to shrug off my paranoia of returning to my provincial roots, I felt extremely self-conscious. Added to that, this was not my subject any more. I'd bullshat my way through the interview trying to get them to hire me.

'We simply don't offer any courses in creative writing,' the administrator had said.

Perhaps she took pity on my dejected face, for she said, 'But we are looking for someone to teach English literature. Do you have any experience?'

I hadn't taught literature for a while, but it didn't stop me from offering myself up to be slaughtered by a room full of freshmen. Till this day, I don't know why I did it. I didn't need the money so bad that I sold my soul. Perhaps I just needed the distraction. Or perhaps there was some greater will at play: that thing with feathers … hope, is it?

A week later, I found myself in a room full of students of varying shapes and sizes. All women, I noted. Different skin tones in different modes of dress, from shalwar suits to tracksuit bottoms, all gazing down at me as if I was about to sprout some piece of prophetic revelation that would change their lives forever.

'Hello there,' I managed to squeak, and the air went out of their expectant faces replaced by an *I knew it* look of disgust. Bored, distracted faces stared back at me and beyond me as I droned on about literary movements in the Romantic era. I could hear the shakiness in my voice.

One girl got up and left the class. Later, in the admin office, I saw two more walk in, their agitated faces betraying their intention to drop the course.

I felt like I'd hit rock bottom, and that I couldn't get any lower. But I was wrong. I came home to my flat share with two graduate students, which was as low as it gets. Thankfully, the students were away on an exchange semester and I had the flat to myself. I stepped in to find a postcard from my husband sitting on top of a pile of bills. It showed the warm Mediterranean Sea with its azure blue waters and cloudless skies. I stared out of the window at the grey Leicester landscape, the grizzly cold sky overwhelmingly dull, and felt lonelier than ever.

I'd take him back right now if he showed up, I remember thinking.

Since I taught part-time and only had two classes a week, the rest of the week, I worked at the university library. I had to. Teaching alone, and that too part-time, doesn't pay the bills. Neither does writing. A dull nine-to-five was needed, and I considered myself lucky it was at the check-in of a library and not the check-outs of a supermarket. The library at Leicester Uni wasn't a particularly busy place. Books and bookshelves seemed out of fashion now that digital had made everything accessible. But every now and then, I'd see a few people come in looking for a quiet place to plug in their laptops or charge their phones, so they could chat with their friends online instead of face to face. Sometimes I'd spot students from the class I taught, but they never said hello. Except one. *The girl with no face*, I used to call her in my head. She was covered from top to toe in a tent-like garment she called the jilbab. *Mother to the hijab?*

I mostly ignored her until, one day, I simply couldn't.

'*Things I've Been Silent About*.'

I looked up to see her dark eyes peering at me through the thin, narrow slit in her veil. She was leaning over the library counter, boring into me with that intense gaze of hers. I couldn't see much of her face but I sensed she was smiling. *It was unnerving.*

'Author?' I said, punching in the library catalogue code on the prehistoric desktop.

The girl remained silent.

'Who's it by?' I repeated, and she looked disappointed. Correction: her eyes seemed disappointed.

'Nafisi.'

I punched a few more buttons on the computer. The search came up blank.

'Sorry,' I said, hoping she would go away and let me work in peace on my new novel that had still to reveal its plot to me.

'*Reading Lolita in Tehran*?' she asked hopefully.

Is she plucking these names out of the air? I thought as the search came up blank again.

'Look,' I said. 'We simply don't have these foreign titles. At least not in this small, provincial library,' I added softly.

It was meant to be a joke, but she looked crushed. Her eyes dimmed and her head stooped. I was fascinated. *Could eyes really be so expressive?* Talking to her required a whole new set of communication, coded through body language. And now, as she stood there slumped against the counter, I felt a surge of pity for her. I wanted to pat her back and say, 'There, there.' Strange, since I hardly knew her. Why should I have cared?

Over the next few days, I got to know her well. Saira – or the veiled one, as I referred to her in my thoughts – was a strange and lonesome girl. She wasn't strange in an obnoxious way but more in an eccentric fashion. She never spoke much but still managed to make her presence felt. Whenever she was around me, she was so quiet that I couldn't help but pay attention to her, whether I wanted to or not. Somehow, I was always conscious of her presence. Sometimes it was the rustling of her silken veil, or the sound of her breath as it knocked against the barriers of her veil escaping in a whistle-like manner. At first glance, she appeared the quiet and studious type, but closer inspection revealed a streak of mischief in her.

I once caught her making patterns on the glass table in the library with her breath, only her nostrils escaping her veil. Once she tried to lift the flap of her veil by exhaling through her mouth. Crazy little eccentricities I found endearing. On an impulse, I ordered her the Iranian books she enquired about daily, as if things could change so quickly.

'Don't get your hopes up,' I told her as she approached me with more impossible names, 'but I have ordered the *Reading Lolita in Tehran* book for you. It'll take time, alright?'

She nodded eagerly, the sides of her veil flapping like the ears of a terrier.

'Look, I don't even know if the library committee will approve it. I had to say many students asked for it, though it was just you.'

She seemed nervous that I had to lie and, for a minute, I was taken aback. *What's a little white lie?* I thought to myself.

As if reading my thoughts, she quoted Shakespeare, 'What a tangled web we weave...'

'Would you rather I didn't?' I interjected.

'No!' she squealed, delighted that her choice of books may actually make it to the shelves here, where Dan Brown and India Knight were the only popular authors.

'I'm sure once the kids read her, they would regret not doing so earlier,' she said with a conviction that was contagious.

Something about her enthusiasm infected me. That night when I went home, I actually prepared my lecture.

The next day, I caught my class off-guard as instead of the usual Elliot and Frost, I threw names at them they had never heard before. Contrary to my expectations, they lapped it up. The girls were curious. Hungry. They wanted more. As my lectures became more innovative, my popularity grew.

The next time Saira came up to the library information desk, I asked her a question before she could ask me any. Unfortunately, it was not one she was expecting. 'Would you like to go for a coffee after my shift?' I asked. It was hard to gauge the expression in her eyes.

Outside, it was bitterly cold. The damp, grey landscape seemed even more bleak as we left the warm glow of the library and walked towards a small, dingy grease spoon cafe off campus. Inside, the smell of fried bacon greeted us warmly and I looked worriedly at Saira. *Shit*, I thought, *would she mind*? Worse, what if it's taken as some sort of Islamophobic attack? But she seemed to be playing that game where she parted her lips slightly and sucked in the mouth flap of her veil, the cloth rising and falling as she drew the fabric in and out with her breath. I watched in fascination till an agitated waitress barked, 'Tea or coffee?'

'Tea, please,' I said, looking expectantly at Saira. But she was busy looking at her feet. My gaze followed. I scraped my chair back to see her swinging her legs back and forth and it was then that I noticed. Her shoes.

Jesus Christ superstar, I almost said aloud, for her kinky boots were hardly what I'd expect her to have on underneath her long flowing body-length veil. Little electric shocks pinged through me. I don't know what I had expected, but those sexy boots were certainly not what I paired with someone who observed strict purdah. I caught her staring at me staring at the thin metal pencil heels and the metal studs around the boot's toe, and I felt the colour rise up my cheeks. I couldn't quite decide why I had expected her shoes to be as inconspicuous as the rest of her. There was nothing in Islam about appropriate footwear, was there? No, I chided myself, it was the stereotype of the submissive veiled woman who had no taste or choice of her own that had kicked in. I'd just assumed women who wore the veil also wore boring old sensible shoes. My bad. Who knew what went on behind those tents these girls wore anyway?

'Well,' the waitress said, breaking into my thoughts. 'Anything for her?'

I felt more heat rise up my face, annoyed that she wouldn't address Saira directly.

She can speak, you know, I wanted to say, but suddenly realized that perhaps Saira didn't want to engage with someone so obviously rude and potentially racist.

'Saira?' I asked. 'Would you like a hot drink?'

She shook her head, magically procuring a thermos out of her long cloak-like jilbab.

'No outside food or beverage,' the rude waitress barked.

I had had enough. Rising to my feet, I said, 'Let's go.'

Saira got up without a word. Almost as if she were expecting it.

I wondered if she got this treatment often.

'Let's go to my house,' I said, haltingly. But she nodded again in that compliant, trustworthy way, as if she had total faith in my ability to end all wars and restore peace.

At home, Saira walked around looking at everything like she was in a museum. She'd pause before a photograph or a bookshelf and observe it like an artefact, her hands holding her chin, her brow creased deep in thought. It was almost comical.

'So tell me,' I said, handing her a cup of steaming hot chocolate, 'where did you develop your taste in world literature?'

'I'm part of that world.'

'Excuse me,' I wondered if she had misheard me.

'It's the world I inhabit.'

I realized that she was trying to tell me that she could relate to it. I leaned back and looked intently at her. 'Were you born here?'

She shook her head. 'Came at age nine.'

'From?'

At this, she got up and started looking at my things again.

I persisted, 'Are you from Pakistan?'

She shook her head.

'Well?'

She turned around suddenly and, from the irritation in her eyes, I felt she was offended by the question. She was obviously as British as I was, having lived here for so long.

But it turned out that's not what was bothering her.

'Iran,' she replied, looking at her cuticles with great scrutiny.

'Ah, so the veil is compulsory.'

'No,' she said simply.

'What do you mean?'

She came and sat opposite me. 'I like it.'

'What do you mean?' I repeated, feeling much like a parrot.

Again that dark, piercing look, the shine in her pupils which made me sense that she was smiling behind her veil, as she said, 'Did you ever read those books as a kid where you got the power to become invisible?'

I laughed. 'Your veil draws more attention than a woman in a bikini.'

'Yes, perhaps. But still. Inside, it's my own little private world. No one knows what I look like, what I wear, how I style my hair...'

'So, are you saying it makes you feel powerful?

She didn't reply and I didn't press her.

By Christmas, we had become almost friends. As different as we were, I enjoyed talking to Saira. And that is what it usually was. Me talking and her listening. There was a stillness to her, a quality I found – as a child-free woman with a marriage that was falling apart and career prospects which were going nowhere – soothing. In the midst of a life sans distractions, Saira's quiet contentment provided a sort of comic relief. The way she simplified everything, the way everything was split into good and evil, her black-and-white view of life was almost refreshing. Little things, when she pointed them out, made me sit up. Once, at a quick stop at the corner shop as I picked out a few things, examining the labels for omega fatty acid, vitamins, iron and all those others that we were supposed to consume to get our five-a-day, Saira asked me why we focussed so much on what was missing than what was present. Her question pertained to food, of course, but for me it summed up life. At times like these, I found it hard to believe that she was only nineteen. Sometimes, her philosophical musings would make me reflect that life didn't have to be so complicated; at other times, they would irk me, for they forced me to rethink my choices in life. Like at this particular moment.

'You can reach conclusions only by the process of elimination, Saira,' I said, handing her the basket as I marched off to the off-licence section. I placed a bottle of wine in the basket knowing full well that it made her uneasy even to be holding an object that carried within it a forbidden drink. Feeling merciful, I took it back from her and marched off to the cashier. 'Stay,' I ordered without looking back, enjoying the power I seemed to wield even outside the classroom. When I turned around, she was gone.

I can't say I wasn't disappointed. Her black cloak felt like a shadow, constant and comforting, attached yet detached. I trudged out of the store feeling bad about pushing the line, only to find her waiting outside. We walked to mine in silence.

It was past ten by the time we reached my flat. Eerily dark and spookily quiet. 'Don't your parents worry?' I asked. She surprised me by saying she lived in the girls' dorm. Her parents had gone back to the old country for a wedding. The statement was jarring. I hadn't quite pictured her as the independent type. For some reason, I expected her to have a pair of smothering parents, a set of authoritarian immigrant grandparents, a few bossy siblings. I felt as if all my estimations were being crushed effectively.

'Does your mum wear the hijab?' I asked as we entered my flat.

'Would it make her a better mum if she did?'

'What an odd question,' I responded.

'So was yours.'

I turned around to look at her, thinking, that was Saira for you. Everything was a riddle. Albeit, I conceded, a simple one.

The more I got to know her, the more my interest in her world grew. I picked up a few of the titles she had suggested and surprised myself. I enjoyed them. Perhaps it was inevitable, but I began to take more interest in my work. As Saira introduced me to more world literature, my lectures became more innovative, so much so that by January, there was a waiting list for my course.

We began to talk every night via texts. Sometimes till late in the night. I got up in the mornings without enough rest, puffy dark circles under my eyes registering their protest. The topic was often me and my failed marriage or my failed career as a writer. I found myself opening up to her, telling her about my string of successful failures. I had managed to get a book deal but it had bombed badly. I hadn't been able to believe my luck at first when it had got published without the usual one hundred rejections that writers were supposed to go through. Later, I could not believe my bad luck.

Saira's reaction to all my issues was, as always, simple. A lack of faith was how she justified it. And after lecturing her on the rubbishness of theology, I would often wonder if there might perhaps just be a wee bit of truth to what she said. It was true, after all, that I had a hard time believing my good fortune, thinking myself undeserving of becoming a published author so easily, and perhaps that is what had manifested itself. A lack of faith ... it got me thinking. If I had believed, truly believed that I deserved success, would I have ended up in this lonely student flat? For a change, taking responsibility instead of blaming others and circumstances seemed to make sense. In fact, the more I got to know Saira, the more I realized how comforting her black-and-white world was, uncomplicated and untouched as it was by the complexities of colour. *I guess sometimes colour can throw you off kilter.*

And so I found myself taking refuge in Saira's black-and-white world, where she was a constant. Wrapped in her trademark black veil, with only a slit for the eyes, quiet and reticent, always ready to listen, Saira seemed almost other-worldly. And perhaps that is why somewhere along the way the boundaries blurred. The day her hug lasted a tad longer, I let it go. But slowly I began to notice the lingering touches, the accidental bumping and the sitting too closely. It didn't take much to figure out that Saira wanted more than just a friendship. *What I didn't realize then was that her love was unconditional.*

She was over the day my husband came back. He walked in unannounced as if he had never left. He wanted to discuss 'us'. Saira made no move to leave. Instead, she asked us if we would like some tea, almost as if we were the guests visiting her house. I have to admit that even I was surprised by her behaviour. Usually, she was shy and reticent around strangers, but at this moment, she seemed more in control of the situation than we were. She made small talk, laying down cups of tea and a plate of biscuits without seeming obviously inquisitive, though I could see she was itching to know what we would say to each other.

Finally, I asked her to sit down and, together, as if explaining to a child we did not have, we told her that we were going to get a divorce. It's not your fault, I almost added, before realizing that she wasn't really part of this tableau. But the glass-shattering look in Saira's eyes seemed to signal that she might as well have been. 'Life is like that,' I said, gently patting her knee, confused at her emotional reaction.

My husband seemed embarrassed by this new project I had taken on, and made his displeasure apparent by rolling his eyes. He may as well have shouted it out. *Freak*, his look seemed to say. She started staring unblinkingly at him through the gap in her veil, and I could see he was becoming more and more edgy by Saira's silent presence. He got up abruptly, saying he would call. He never did.

But that did not stop Saira from enquiring again, and yet again, if he had called. A strange sort of anxiety reflected in her eyes every time I told her that the only news I had of him was through his Facebook newsfeed of mutual friends. I'm not sure whether she was more shocked at the looming divorce or at the fact that he had unfriended me on Facebook. Either way, she blamed herself.

For the next few weeks, she showed up every day with baked goods or old second-hand copies of books she thought I might like. Her charity irked me. It made me feel pitied. Disturbing when, if anything, I was relieved that this sagging old chapter of my life had finally closed. I could start afresh. But what I thought was a fresh start, Saira regarded as rejection.

I still remember the hurt look in her eyes when she showed up unexpectedly one night at my house and found me getting ready for a date.

'But you can't,' she cried out, a piercing shrillness to her voice.

I turned around to look at her devastated face and knew instantly that this had gone on far too long. Her neediness was appalling.

Cruel as it was, I knew what I had to do next. 'Kill your darlings', an expression I used in my creative writing classes when telling students to cut out words that didn't fit into the story, came to mind, as I walked up to her. I held her firmly by the shoulders and looked into her eyes. 'Now look, Saira,' I began, but what happened next shook me to the core. It was over in a flash but there was no mistaking the touch of something wet on my lips as Saira leaned into me.

The kiss lasted barely a second. I stepped back. I had taken her neediness as a longing for something maternal. It never crossed my mind that the touching could have been sexual. Saira took my surprise for disgust and ran into the night, almost tripping over her long black cloak. Her face, I noticed, was still uncovered.

Though I still met the guy I had hooked up with on the dating app, my entire being felt numb. I kept forgetting his name, was restless, and the whole date was over in less than an hour. If the evening was a disaster, the night was even worse, for I kept thinking about the softness of the encounter, the unexpectedness of it all. But I suppose what was really bothering me was that I was considering the possibility.

I had trouble concentrating the next day, too. Everything irritated me. I couldn't wait for the day to be over. I went through the motions, teaching as if on auto-pilot, coming home, watching *EastEnders* robotically, going through the pretence of dinner, till finally I couldn't take the deafening silence any more. I dialled her number.

Correction, I kept dialling her number.

Without Saira and her flowing black cloak, her curious eyes barely visible through the thin slit in her veil, the day seemed long. I hadn't noticed how habituated I had become to her presence. I missed her. If only to have someone to talk to. Or rather someone listening to me talking. I walked by the café, the library, searched for her face – her veil, rather – in the classroom. But it was as if she had never existed. In fact, it was almost as if I had made her up. *Had she really existed?*

It didn't help that there was no record of her at the girls' dorm. Just when I was about to admit she had been an imaginary friend, I managed to get her real address from the admin office. But once I had it in my hands, I didn't know what to do. I hadn't thought it through. No, I admitted, as I looked it up on Google Maps, I had no idea what I was doing, for wasn't the intention to roll back? To have less of her in my life? Less, yes, but not complete desertion, I argued with myself. I remember pausing at the bus station and wondering if I would have felt the same way had it been me who had cut off all contact with her.

As I stepped onto the bus heading to her neighbourhood, I convinced myself that it had nothing to do with the kiss. Lately, I had become pretty good at that – convincing myself otherwise, that is. Guess it comes with practice. The word 'self-denial' didn't even cross my mind. I told myself that I just needed to make sure she was okay. The girl was confused, I assured myself as I rang her bell.

I looked around as I waited on the porch. The neighbourhood she lived in was at the edge of town, completely ethnic, and I felt almost foreign as the only white female and that too in a skirt.

There were skinny brown children playing in the yards, and the houses had open windows from which wafted smells of curries and freshly made chapattis.

My stomach growled and a bearded man passing by stopped to look at me. When I smiled and said hello, he hurried away almost as if I had made a pass at him. I rang the bell again. This time leaving my hand on the buzzer for a good one minute.

After much knocking – I don't know why I was convinced she was home – the door flew open. An angry Saira stood in the doorway, her head uncovered, her face in a frown and, most shockingly, her feet bare.

'What do you want?' she said, her voice low and gruff.

'Why are you missing class?' I placed my hand firmly on the door, in case she intended to slam it on my face. 'Look, if it's because of me,' I continued, 'then really, don't do this to yourself.'

She continued to stare sullenly at her feet.

'Look, Saira, can we talk?'

She let out a long, slow breath. 'Come in,' she said, and padded inside. I followed.

Inside, the walls were bare except for a few pictures of mosques. They were painted a dark greenish-blue with egg-yolk borders. The flaky and chipped paint made it seem as if you were underwater – drowning.

Depressing, I remember thinking.

'So this is a little different than the girls' dorm ...' I began, but seeing her stiffen, I realized how accusatory I sounded.

'Saira, I just want to know what's going on with you. All these lies...'

'Get out,' she shouted.

I stood still.

'Okay, don't tell me why you lied about where you live. Just tell me why you are not coming to class. Is it because of me?'

For a good five minutes, she said nothing and then suddenly a barrage of words flowed from her. 'Look, the real reason I'm not attending class is because I want to go to Pakistan and get married.'

'I thought you were from Iran?' I asked, barely able to decide what took priority – the discrepancies and lies or the threat of an arranged marriage.

'I lied,' she said flatly. 'My parents are immigrants from Punjab. I thought Iran sounded more exciting.'

I just opened and shut my mouth till, finally, I decided to focus on the issue at hand instead of the string of lies. I managed to say, 'Are they forcing you into an arranged marriage?'

'I wish,' she laughed bitterly.

'Okay,' I said. 'I need to sit down.'

'Sofa ain't got no spikes, bitch,' she said with a shrug and all I could do was stare at her. Her entire body language, her demeanour, her speech, everything had changed. *Who is the real Saira,* I wondered, *this girl in sweats who swears, or the veiled girl whose politeness is almost Victorian?*

'Fucking, sit down,' she said as she, to my horror, lit a cigarette.

'Wow,' I said. 'Quite a bit you lied about.'

'Well, I didn't lie about this,' she said as she suddenly lunged at me and shoved her tongue down my throat.

'What's wrong with you?' I shouted, shoving her away, only to see she was in tears.

'Saira, Saira, oh my dear,' I said, sitting down next to her as her whole body racked with sobs. 'Look, you are confused. It's okay. We all go through these phases where we are confused about our sexuality. I think you are misinterpreting affection for desire,' I said, patting her head gently.

'I'm not confused,' she said through the tears.

'Look, I don't think you are a lesbian, frankly. I think you are just confused. But even if you were, it's okay to have feelings for the same sex, really...'

'No,' she shouted. 'It's not okay. It's haram.'

'Oh Saira...'

'Just shut it,' she said, putting up her hand. 'You don't understand. No one does. Even I don't. I've...I've got feelings for other women. I'm...I'm a fucking freak. That's why I want to get married. I want an arranged marriage. Back in Pakistan.'

I felt like a mother whose architect daughter had told her she wants to design dog kennels. 'Why?' I burst out. 'Why the fuck do you want to throw your life away? Just because your bloody Islam doesn't accept homosexuality?'

Then, seeing the look on her face as she crumpled the cigarette, I forced myself to calm down. 'Look, Saira, I didn't mean it to come out like that.'

'I want an arranged marriage,' she repeated like an errant child demanding a new toy.

I took a deep inhale and said, 'And what do your parents think?'

'My mother doesn't think much.'

I ignored the sarcasm and said, 'Your father, then?'

'My father left us way back.'

'Oh.' Suddenly, the neediness for acceptance made sense. As did her reaction to the break-up of my marriage. 'I'm sorry,' I said, 'You never mentioned...'

'That's because you never asked. You're always going on about your own bloody life.'

I felt heat rise to my face but swallowed my anger and focused on her. 'And what does your mother say about the "arranged marriage"?' I raised my fingers to quote unquote.

'My mother thinks an "arranged marriage",' she raised two fingers to mimic me, 'is too costly. She doesn't have money for the dowry.'

The surprise on my face must have given me away, for she continued, 'My mum works ten hours in the factory down the road. She says it's too expensive to buy tickets to Pakistan, then get all the gifts for the relatives, find a match, and then pay for the overseas wedding. "Why can't you just find a nice boy here and settle down" were my mum's words to me, can you imagine?'

No, I can't, I almost said, as yet another stereotype of the Muslim immigrant was shattered before me.

'Saira,' I said as I put my hands on my knees to get up. 'I think you really need to do some serious thinking. Please just promise me you won't rush into anything. Life is not as black and white as religion makes it out to be. I've heard so many stories of disastrous arranged marriages...'

She got up so suddenly that I had to step back. 'For you, everything is a bloody story,' she almost spat out the words and I backed away further, frightened by this side of hers.

We stared at each other for a good few minutes before I finally stepped aside. Before leaving, I turned around and said, 'You know, in some ways, yes, I do think that. Everything is a story. And we are all made up of stories. Stories that we tell others, stories we tell ourselves and stories that we don't want anyone to know.'

She was quiet as she took it in and I took that moment to hug her. Her thin body felt warm. Warm and welcoming. For a second I was reminded of the smell of home, of wet earth, of the vibrant green grass after the rains, of talcum powder and the smells of freshly baked bread. I hugged her harder, and suddenly it felt as if I had stepped in front of a bus all over again. I breathed it all in before pulling away.

'Goodbye, Saira,' I said.

Of all the goodbyes I had to face recently, I knew this one was the most painful. And also the most necessary.

These days I find myself wondering if this is a story I want to tell or one I want to forget. I wasn't proud of myself for walking away. But I also knew that it was dangerous to let Saira's infatuation fester. It would have led to no good, I told myself every time something reminded me of her. Yet, I couldn't help wondering what would have happened if I had ... if I had kissed her back. *Why had I resisted so much?*

The episode with Saira had made me more reflective. But also sedate. I didn't lose my temper any more, but my lectures lost their spark as well. I went back to teaching the Dead White Males and their so-called classics instead of experimenting with world literature. It was safe. And I needed the safety of the familiar. I moved further away towards the highlands where sameness was cherished, difference feared.

Every time I saw a girl in a hijab, which was rare in those parts, I was reminded of Saira and her curious gaze, her simple ways. I often wondered why I had been so angry with her. Or so afraid of her. Of her sexuality. Of her beliefs. I had been so convinced that I was right, that my way was the only way. The digging in of heels seemed ridiculous now. Why couldn't I accept that someone could want an arranged marriage, or that they can be happy veiled head to toe? Why was I so afraid to accept her as she really was? Or perhaps I was afraid to accept my own feelings for her. Maybe what I felt for her was just a little more than maternal affection. But I had chosen to block all feelings. To close off, abandon and desert. To run, to hide.

Had I really been much different from my husband in the way I had acted? What if I had sat down with her when she had calmed down? Would she have explained everything patiently in one of our late-night chats? Would I have listened? But it was too late now. I imagined her sitting somewhere in Pakistan, in a hut brimming with relatives, a little one on her knee, and I winced. But then I told myself, Saira was a survivor. Perhaps she had made peace with herself instead of with her headscarf.

I smiled. And somewhere across the ocean, I was sure Saira was smiling back.

Under the Flyover

It was a sight to behold. The half-constructed, half-demolished flyover on Sharah-i-Faisal looked as if it been bombed during an air raid, the iron spikes jutting out from the half-finished stretches on either side like the desperate outstretched fingers of two lovers reaching out to each other before meeting an untimely end. The broken columns on each end of the flyover pierced the sky with spikes that looked like thin needles gathering rust. And the blue sky trapped between these columns looked like an intruder who had been caught by the sun's fierce glare. Creating this mental picture, Shahid stepped back, satisfied.

A few years ago, he would have whipped out his notebook or phone and jotted down these thoughts, but now ... now things were different. He had responsibilities now. And thinking of responsibilities, he glanced at his watch. It was a quarter past five and Shumaila still hadn't emerged from her office across the road. He looked across the broken flyover towards the tall steel-

and-glass building which looked as out of place, framed by rubbish and swarmed by flies, as he felt in his nine-to-five job. With his poetic sensibilities, he would much rather have led a life of poverty as an artist, but he knew that was not an option any more. Not when his parents had invested so much in his education, sending him to a private school instead of the local government school where his elder brothers had studied. As if that was not enough, they had paid hefty bribes to get him a job as a junior accountant in a private firm. No, he could not let them down. But he could let go of his love for poetry.

'*Hazaron khawahishein aisi ...*' he sighed, quoting Ghalib, and then shook his head as a day-labourer stopped to ask if he was addressing him. He looked again at the beautiful, if misplaced, skyscraper across the road where Shumaila worked as a receptionist and then back again at his watch. 'Aati hi hogi,' he said again to no one in particular, as he climbed back onto his skinny motorbike.

Shahid watched the sea of vehicles crawl slowly under the blockage of the construction and remarked, 'What havoc these flyovers have caused all over the city.' A stray cat froze at the boom of his voice and ran off when he heaved an even louder sigh. The futility of these roads and flyovers, which creaked under the weight of Karachi's ever-increasing barrage of cars, seemed to him a useless exercise. *Like throwing good money after bad*, he thought. They reminded him of the hordes of half-empty flats that dotted the city's skyline, their construction halted midway because of some judicial stay order or the other. These flats with their hollow, glassless windows, reminded him of a vertically stretched skull with hundreds of dark empty sockets for eyes. He shook his head, reflecting that nothing in this city ever reached a conclusion. Everything was just starting out or being broken down. There was constant turmoil. 'No planning,' he said aloud to an imaginary audience. 'No planning at all in this Karachi of ours.'

He shook his head as he glanced again at the still doors of the building. And then, as he waited for Shumaila to emerge, he thought this sort of short-sightedness and impulsiveness was not only the city's character but also that of its inhabitants. He himself had jumped into this relationship without thinking. But was he solely to blame...

Before he could ponder more, he saw Shumaila finally exit the building. He watched her cross the road, dodging bikes and zigzagging her way through the slow-moving cars in the bumper-to-bumper traffic. He knew she would step onto the busy road instead of using the overhead bridge further down. That was another useless afterthought! *Do the idiots in charge really think someone would climb two-hundred steps to get to the other side of the road when they could just squeeze through the gap in the fence separating the traffic?* Shahid smiled at the thought.

'They really don't understand Pakistaniyat,' he said, this time directly addressing the cat that had slowly inched her way back to the pile of rubbish next to his bike.

He got up abruptly, scaring the feline again as he began to wave vigorously across the road.

Shumaila's hijab was tightly wound around her head and her dusty face seemed to sweat profusely, now that she was no longer in her air-conditioned office. But the scowl on her face was replaced immediately by a smile when she saw him waving at her. In the cloud of smoke and dust that arose all around her, Shahid thought she seemed almost like an apparition. The hour-long wait was forgotten and he geared up his bike, the broken flyovers and garbage around him replaced by flowers and Bollywood-style gardens in his imagination.

She climbed on shyly and they joined the swarm of vehicles on the road, zigzagging their way towards the park where they spent most evenings. Once they crossed Metropole, Shahid left the stream of traffic and parked in a narrow, unpaved alley, which seemed even more dug-up than the site of the half-bombed, half-built flyover.

Before getting off the bike, he pulled her close and gave her a quick peck on the cheek. Shumaila giggled and shrank back with a rhetorical, 'Koi dekh lega'.

'Let them see,' Shahid laughed, even though his eyes darted about furiously to see if indeed anyone had seen them. The lane looked deserted. He grew bolder. He took her hand and pulled her close. But just as he leaned towards her, his phone rang.

'Beta, ghar kab aao gey?' his mother's shrill voice rang out. He looked at Shumaila, who looked away, a sour expression on her face.

'I'll be home soon, Ami,' he said and hung up.

'Sorry,' he said sheepishly, for by now, a few men with shovels had entered the pebbly lane. He parked his bike and they made their way through the workmen digging up the already dug-up road.

'This city is constantly being dug up,' Shahid said as he led her towards the green, leafy gardens of Frere Hall.

Shumaila scowled some more and said, 'I wouldn't mind if they actually fixed it, but they just dig up roads and leave them like that. The whole city looks like a colony of giant molehills, with streams of ants swarming around it.'

Shahid smiled at the image but said nothing. He knew these conversations only made her more irate, and that somehow the mismanagement of the city would eventually become the fault of his mother and sister, who seemed to be responsible for most of Shumaila's troubles in the world.

Away from the smoke and exhaust, and under the green shade of the former church, Shumaila's mood lifted and she reached for his hand. Out of habit, he glanced around for pesky policemen who preferred troubling couples to controlling crime. Seeing no one around, he squeezed her hand back. His mobile rang again. This time it was a request from his younger sister to buy milk and eggs on his way home.

'Can't you turn it off?' Shumaila asked, the irritation rising in her voice.

He laughed and said, 'You want them to send out a search party?'

'Just tell them you are with me.'

Shahid looked as if she had told him to go jump in a well.

'How long will we hide? I mean how can your family be so ... so ...' Shumaila was about to say inconsiderate when she thought better of it and turned away.

'Shumaila, listen, I know ...' Shahid's voice trailed off as his phone rang again.

Without glancing at the screen, he shouted, 'What the hell now?'

A smiling Shumaila watched as Shahid's defiant expression changed into an apologetic one.

'Sir,' he mumbled, 'Sorry, sir, I thought ... yes, yes, sir. Jee, sir, I...'

He looked up at her with pleading eyes and whispered, 'Five minutes?' Then, without waiting for an answer, he turned away and started taking notes.

As soon as he hung up, he stuffed his notepad into his shirt pocket and grabbed her hand. He held it close to her heart. The weather was hot and there were very few people about. The couple moved closer. They didn't need words as their hands pawed each other hungrily. The roar of a motorcycle made them jump apart and they looked up just in time to see a man approaching on foot.

'Coffee, tea, sir?' the man asked.

'Nahin,' Shahid said, but the man refused to go away. They knew there was no restaurant here and this was just a ploy to harass couples. Not wanting to waste precious time arguing with the man, Shahid pulled out a fifty-rupee note and waved him away. But it was too late. The man had seen his wallet and now refused to leave them alone.

'Let's go,' Shahid said, getting up abruptly and motioning her to follow him.

The man began whistling and singing lewd songs as she got up and dusted the back of her abaya. Shumaila glared at him.

'Don't engage,' Shahid said, grabbing her hand and pulling her away. The sun was setting and he thought it better to leave. They made their way back to the alley where they had parked. But it wasn't their day. The sky darkened and a crunching noise on the gravelly road made their steps falter. A police patrol had turned into the lane.

As the white-and-blue police pickup truck slowly and ominously made its way towards them, Shahid's heart sank. He realized the guy harassing them must have been an informer.

'Where to, Romeo?' A portly policeman emerged from the beat-up mobile and grabbed Shahid by the shoulder.

'Let go,' he said, although every instinct told him not to.

'Oye, ankhen dikhata hai? I'll put you in the lock-up and see how much you raise your voice then.'

'The police in Karachi has no crime to fight that you are always patrolling parks?' Shumaila asked.

'Madam seems very experienced,' the policeman sniggered, and a hot fever of colour burst onto Shahid's face.

'Chalo,' he said to Shumaila, getting on the bike.

'Oye, wait, oye,' the policeman said, snatching his helmet away. 'Where do you think you are going? Tell me your addresses and your parents' phone numbers.'

The couple exchanged a brief look.

'I said—'

'Flat number 1300, Cage Building, Cantt,' Shahid said with a sudden impatience.

Slightly irked at getting the information so easily, the man barked, 'And the laadeez' address?'

'Same.'

For a second, the pot-bellied policeman looked confused. He narrowed his beady little eyes at them and then, as if some sort of enlightenment had dawned upon him, asked, 'Cousins?'

'No,' Shahid said with as much patience as he could muster up.

'Don't act smart with me,' the policeman leaned right into him. 'If you care so much about her reputation, why bring her here?'

'Because she is my wife,' Shahid shouted at him.

'Wife?' Now it was the policemen's turn to exchange looks.

The one with the protruding belly gave himself a good scratch before roughly shoving Shahid in the chest, 'Acha, so show me your nikahnama,' he said, to which Shumaila quickly pulled out a copy which had their NICs stapled across it.

The man snatched it while staring at her with so much loathing that she had to look away.

He spat as he turned the document over in his hands, trying to match the names on the NIC with the form. Convinced there was no loophole to dive into, he waved the document over their heads and shouted, 'Oye, then why are you acting like lovers if you are married?'

The couple considered the irony of the man's words and decided to stay silent.

The trimmer one of the two policemen now stepped up: 'What are you wasting our time for, then? Why go to a park if you are married? Go home and do what you want to do!'

'We can't,' Shumaila said, turning her face away as if disgraced by the weight of her own words.

The policemen twirled their moustaches and turned expectantly towards the boy: 'Why? Why can't you go home?'

A loud exhale followed before Shahid said, 'Sir, because our lives are like the broken flyover.'

'Hain jee?' The pot-bellied policeman scratched his bald head again and said, 'What flyover?'

'The half-constructed, half-demolished one.'

Their confusion had now reached pitiful heights, so the boy explained, 'You see, they built it without thinking, then tried to demolish it without thinking. Our parents got us married because I had got a job, but they never thought about where we would live. First they couldn't wait to get us married, now they constantly try to keep us apart.'

The policeman and his subordinate stared at them blankly, still unable to comprehend what the problem was.

'Jee,' Shumaila added, 'like the flyover, our parents rushed us into marriage but didn't think what marriage meant. They never realized that there was no space for us in the house. They never thought about privacy, intimacy ...' her voice trailed off. Clearing her throat, she continued, 'We come here because we have no place to sit and talk. We are interrupted all the time. At night, we share a room with his younger sisters.'

Shahid dropped his head and said, 'We never even get a chance to *talk* alone in our two-bedroom flat, let alone...'

As if on cue, his phone rang. It was his sister asking him not to forget the eggs and milk.

When he hung up, he did not think it was worth his while completing his sentence.

'Chalo,' he said to Shumaila. 'Hurry.'

'Yes,' she nodded bitterly, 'the eggs and milk can't be kept waiting.'

The policemen let them go with a sense of paternal understanding.

'Eggs and milk,' the beleaguered couple heard the men tut-tut as they roared past and joined the sea of motorbikes, rickshaws and cars jostling along on Karachi's half-dug-up and half-constructed roads.

In just a few minutes, they were indistinguishable in the swarm of similar couples on narrow bikes, all disappearing into a cloud of cement and dust in this broken city.

The Full Stop

Assia put down the Judy Blume novel she had been reading on the pillow next to her. Poking the neatly folded sheets at the end of the bed, she kicked her legs up in the air and stretched the bedsheet over herself. Pulling it over her head, she stuck two fingers into her vagina and then held them up to her nostrils to examine. Her hand smelt strange and unfamiliar. A wave of pain ran through her body and she doubled over.

'Ami,' she cried. But no one came.

Feeling almost nauseated with the sharp jabs of pain that had begun to pierce through her abdomen, she dragged herself to the bathroom. When she got up to flush, her head almost reeled. It had happened. The thing she had read about in books, heard older cousins discuss discreetly, had finally happened to her. Assia felt almost proud of her body.

'Ami,' she ran to the kitchen where her mother stood stirring a pot over a blazing stove.

'Ji, beta?' she responded. Before Assia could reply, Ami pointed towards the carrots. 'Scrape them quickly. It's nearly time for your father to come home.'

Assia ignored her. 'Ami, I got my periods.'

Without looking up, her mother turned off the stove and turned towards her. 'Where?' she asked, instead of the 'when' Assia had expected. She grabbed her arm with an urgency Assia could not understand and began to drag her out of the kitchen.

'I was on the bed, reading...'

Her mother marched her off to the bedroom before she could even complete her sentence. Once there, her mother stripped the bed sheets while telling Assia to take out clean clothes and an old underwear from her cupboard. With robotic efficiency, her mother dumped the sheets and her clothes into the washing machine as she instructed Assia to stay in the bathroom. About five minutes later, her Ami came in with a pad, some cotton and gauze. She instructed Assia to use the pad at first and then, when it got full, to replace it with cotton wool wrapped in gauze. She taught her how to secure it in her underwear.

'Now don't throw it out if it's only half full,' she instructed.

Assia could only blink in response, for she could not imagine the thought of more than a few red dots leaking from her body.

As if reading her thoughts, her mother paused in the middle of wrapping gauze and rubbed her arms. 'Happens,' she murmured.

'Okay,' she said, getting up. 'Now don't pray or touch the Quran in this condition. Don't bathe the first few days. And Assia,' she looked at her sternly, 'beta, keep yourself clean and keep the house clean. I don't want to be wiping spots off the furniture. It will be very embarrassing.'

Slowly, as her mother hurried back to the kitchen, Assia felt a sense of shame creep in; as if she had spilled a drink in front of guests, or she had seen something she wasn't meant to. She walked with slow, hesitant steps back to her bed, the bare mattress staring up at her as if to complain. Not knowing what to do, she spread a couple of newspapers on the bed before covering it with a bed sheet. The papers crunched as she sat down, echoing her discomfort. She ran a hand over the book she had been reading, wondering why the experience of her first period was so different from that of the heroines in her English novels.

Where is the celebration, the big talk, the 'you are a woman now' chat?

Perhaps that stuff was all made up, she mused. A passing thought, as she stared at the fair-skinned girl in a dress on the cover of her book, nagged her: these books are set elsewhere, it seemed to say. These books don't tell your story.

She dismissed it, for she loved Judy Blume. And didn't the blurb say the stories she wrote were universal?

The doorbell rang before she could ponder any further. She jumped up, making the newspapers crackle beneath her, as if reminding her to be careful. She dashed across the hall, then slowed her run into a brisk walk as she neared the door. Opening the door with a flourish, she was about to shout, 'Salaam Alaiqum, Abu', but stopped when she saw the solemn look on his face. Her father stood in the doorway in his white medical coat, his head cocked to one side as he spoke on his cellphone.

'Yes, give her 5ml of paracetamol. Yes, yes, you can call me in an hour if the fever doesn't break. Ji, okay. No problem.'

He walked past her, nodding at her salaam. Assia watched her father as he placed his briefcase on the table and, for the hundredth time, thought how she would much rather be like him and save lives than like her mother, slogging away in the kitchen at all hours. A thin veil of resentment seemed to mask her face as she thought of her mother and her lack of enthusiasm at her big moment. She's probably never read a book in her life, Assia decided with some contempt.

Without thinking, she marched up to her father and said, 'Abba, I have some news.'

'Ji, beta,' her father beamed. 'Did you get first prize in the art competition?'

'No, Abba, but something tremendous happened today. I got my first period.' She waited, secure in the knowledge that her father would explain everything to her in medical terms, for he understood the importance of the momentous thing that had taken place today. In the books, this was a life-transforming event. What should she expect from her body, she wondered as she stared expectantly at him. Wasn't this the boundary that separated girls from women? Wasn't she officially a grown-up now? She stared eagerly up at him, wanting to remember this moment forever. And she did.

Her father seemed to have frozen, his colour a shade darker. His eyes darted from side to side, though his body was still. Finally, after a few seconds, he carried on as if nothing had been said. He cleaned his glasses and turned on the TV, flipping to his favourite talk show host. Then, when she continued to hover over him, he raised the volume. When she still didn't leave, he shouted for his wife. Her mother appeared, face red from the heat of the stove, hands smelling of spices and garlic. Assia looked contemptuously at her. But then she saw him nod towards her and in that momentary wordless exchange, her father's face seemed to transmit a deep sense of embarrassment. Wordlessly, her mother tucked Assia's elbow into the crook of her arm.

'Chalo,' she whispered, gently nudging her out. A confused Assia looked back over her shoulder as her mother draped a dupatta over her and pulled her into the kitchen.

'Come and help me cook.'

Yanking the dupatta off, Assia marched out of the kitchen, only to stop when she saw her father's face. A deep pop of colour seemed to rise from his collar to his cheeks, as if something had exploded in his shirt. His neck seemed to have sunk into his shoulders and he seemed to her, suddenly, older.

She watched her father's face grow more and more distant and she realized that her story would not turn out like that of her American young adult novels. In her story, menstruation was a thing to be hushed, veiled and concealed – not celebrated. It was the moment when honour was replaced by shame, friendship with humiliation, and love by fear. For girls in her part of the world, pads were concealed in brown paper bags like counterfeits, films on the subject were banned, and the denial of a natural state was encouraged. They were called impure, napak and unclean. This was not something to be discussed ... not now, not ever. And so, in that one moment as she saw her father turn away from her and her mother in denial, Assia found clarity. She knew now why it was called the period. Because, like a full stop, this moment in a girl's life put an end to all conversations.

Period.

The Girl Who Split in Two

I draw a line. Straight down the middle of the photo. Between her eyes, down her nose, across her mouth, dividing her chin into neat halves. I tear along the line. Tear her in two. I put the right away. I hold onto the left.

I am going to hold it all day.

I can't tear it. I can't frame it. I do what I always do when I don't know what to do. I close my eyes and bury it, deep inside my mouth. I chew slowly, neatly, firmly. But when I open my eyes, she is still there. Except she isn't. Not physically. I find myself thinking that the Old Me, the one that exists only in my past, will never leave me alone.

Time to go. Yallah.

The rusty old van cranks up the mountainous terrain of Palmyra. I imagine the supplies of ammunition inside sliding from one end of the seats to the other like cans of beans rattling down a hill. It was the same bus that had brought me here. From Luton. But that was another life, another me. I soon forget as people rush out of their tents to greet it. The bus is like a bird of hope – it makes you forget your surroundings, if only for a second.

This time it's not bringing people, but supplies. The residents scramble towards it, holding out their hands like beggars. It stands there, majestic in its rusty old body, guns sticking out of the broken windowpanes, sacks of flour sending up clouds of white dust as they unload them along with boxes of grenades. It seems surreal. Like a child's drawing where all sorts of things are jumbled up – nappies next to bombs, and bullets next to bananas.

This is a joke.

The driver unloads a cargo full of the latest arms, and the crowd steps back. That is not what the hopeful want. They are waiting for everyday luxuries like shampoo, soap, toilet paper, sanitary napkins, toothpaste. The Old Me reminds me that these things were not luxuries back home, but necessities. I tell her to be quiet. I'm afraid that someone would hear her.

I don't want to draw attention. Soon, the van would return and those in need of things not supplied on this trip will be allowed to come on board.

The Old Me is already there, waiting.

The driver honks three times. 'Bus will leave soon. Only twenty people. Minimum luggage. No breakables.' I think of all the things that can break.

Promises, hearts, bonds, the news...

'Come on. We have to leave before sunset. Yallah, yallah! I push my way through.

The past is in the past.

I'm usually the first to volunteer for the supplies mission, but even if I get there first, I know it is no guarantee that I would get in. There is much pushing and shoving, hitting and name-calling as people scramble to be one amongst the first twenty. There are eight seats inside and the four to a seat load is stretching to its max already. For a second, the jostling stops and I look up to see Abu Jihad's tall frame approaching. Two guns slung casually over his shoulders, he walks slowly, the crowd parting to let him pass. He is known for his ruthlessness. No one wants to mess with him. He elbows a blind old lady who wanders accidentally into his path, and climbs aboard, riding shotgun. The driver mutters something about women and children boarding first, but his words are lost in the general clamour of people trying to get on or get their lists on to someone they trust. The old lady cries out as someone steps over her foot in the stampede.

Survival of the fittest.

The Old Me makes its way through the sea of people and yanks Abu Jihad out by his long greasy locks. Pushing him to the ground, she puts her foot on his chest and points a Kalashnikov at him. When he tries to resist, she pushes the nozzle into his mouth and threatens to pull the trigger unless he apologizes. Abu Jihad grovels at her feet, begging for mercy. Generously, she lets him go, but not without warning to blow his brains out if he ever pushes an old and helpless woman again.

Of course, the New Me does nothing but watch.

I don't have time to help the old woman. Nobody does. When I finally elbow my way in, I stumble onto the gearbox in the front. My eyes lock for a second with Abu Jihad and he flashes me a leery smile, his gold fillings a stark contrast to the black rot of his teeth. He is covered from head to toe in brands. A Nike cap on his head, Adidas on his feet, Abercrombie and Finch logo on his t-shirt, Guess Jeans, Ray-bans perched on his nose.

He hates the West.

I pull my hijab closer to my skin and hope to get a seat as far away as possible. He is known for his one-night brides. Most of them teenagers.

I'm out of luck. The van is crammed full. Abu Jihad pushes the adolescent boy next to him into the gearbox and makes room for me. As unobtrusively as possible, I slip into the seat and try to disappear.

'Subhan Allah,' Abu Jihad strips me with his eyes as he praises god. His pupils burn through my black niqab and set alight my toe-length abaya.

I feel naked.

He rubs his fleshy lower lip with his thumb and says, 'Get closer, sister.'

Here, everyone is a sister or brother. The word is like the local currency – useful but of little value.

'Sit back, sister. Here, come closer.'

The Old Me slaps him hard and tells him to go fuck himself.

The New Me lowers her gaze.

'You new here, sister?'

I nod mutely.

'Allah, Allah ...' He murmurs softly and I feel my intestines twisting, as if some invisible claw is squeezing my insides. The heat and the acrid smell of sweat in the cramped space add to my nausea. I remember how his last jihadi bride died in childbirth. She too was sixteen.

He leans over me and says something in Arabic to the pasty young boy sitting next to me, his bottom hardly on the seat and his knees knocking against the gear. The boy shifts slightly and Abu Jihad hisses at him again. The boy's face pales. I try to understand what he's saying, but my Arabic is still weak. The boy's neck stoops and his longish hair covers his reddening cheeks.

'I really need to go into town,' he replies in French. 'Please don't make me get off here. I won't be able to find my way back.'

Abu Jihad seems taken aback. I can tell he is not used to being spoken back to, much less disobeyed.

But he also wants to impress me. He's in no mood to pick a fight. Not *that* kind of a fight, at least.

He leans forward, his arm casually brushing against my breasts.

So much for modesty.

'No problem! What is your name, brother?'

'Liam,' the boy replies gratefully. 'My name is Liam, brother.'

'Are you sure?' Abu Jihad slaps the back of his neck, his long arm brushing my face, 'You look like a Lucy to me.'

The people in the seat behind us giggle. The Old Me turns around sharply and admonishes them. *Don't encourage him*, she screams in my head, *you could be next, for all you know.*

The New Me looks down at her feet.

'So Brother Lucy, you kill a man yet? No? You start with chickens.'

The passengers snicker. Liam turns a deep shade of red.

'No guts, huh, Lucy boy?' he slaps his head again.

The Old Me wants to slap his arm away and say, *it's Liam, you jerk. The boy's name is Liam and he's just fifteen. He left his family in Toulouse for your fake Islamist mission, you fraud. You cyber-kidnapper. You hypocrite.*

The New Me holds her breath and hopes to melt back into the steaming-hot leather seats.

'Hey, hey, Brother Lucy,' he teases, 'what's so urgent? Your chest beginning to jiggle? You going to town to buy a bra?'

Giggles run through the van like a tidal wave. Liam's eyes prickle with tears.

'*That's enough!*' The Old Me yanks Abu Jihad's head back and shoves a bra down his throat. *Swallow,* she commands.

'Come on, man, say something,' Abu Jihad roars. 'Cat got your tongue?'

It's an old joke, but the bus laughs, its passengers relieved that the joke is not on them.

Cowards.

The Old Me stands up to shame them.

'Al Hamd ul Allah,' Liam sputters, his voice hushed and uneven like a child speaking through a rolled-up newspaper.

'What say?' Abu Jihad roars and Liam's voice begins to crack.

Abu Jihad throws his head back and laughs. 'You even *sound* like a girl. God got confused in the factory or what! You got both organs, man? Penis and breasts?'

The bus explodes into loud guffaws. Liam's face is so red now that I feel the blood in his head will explode and taint us all scarlet. A vein pulses in his temple.

Why don't you grow a pair?

But there's no stopping Abu Jihad. The man is on a roll.

'You reached the age of consent, man? You'll make someone a great wife someday.'

The bus shakes with laughter as hot tears race down Liam's cheeks. Everyone is laughing except the Old Me, who is glaring at Abu Jihad, chopping him up, slice by slice, with her laser-sharp eyes.

'Or do you prefer goats, man?'

A sob escapes Liam's throat. This tickles the passengers even more.

'Come on, man,' he pulls at Liam's shirt, 'show us.'

'No,' Liam shouts.

The laughter, I notice, is subdued now. The joke is no longer funny.

'Enough, Abu,' the driver says softly. 'He's only a boy.'

Despite the cramped space, Abu Jihad turns his whole body to face the driver.

'Uncle, if he can't take a little teasing, how is he going to take the torture of the Americans?' He leans over and cups Liam's face in his hand. 'They rip out your fingernails for a piece of information, my brother. They poke cigarette butts in your balls, prick pins in your eyes, stick electric wires up your asshole, and you crying about name calling? Toughen up, boy. This ain't a video game.'

Liam's thighs are beginning to tremble and I'm filled with an urge to hold him. I want to press his hand into mine and comfort him. Hug him. And I almost do, but

I feel Abu Jihad's eyes on me, his breath hot on my face. A scalding rush surges up my body, making my heart beat itself into a mad frenzy as I realize I've just become visible. My poised hand sneaks back into the long folds of my abaya.

What are you even doing here?

The Old Me stares back at Abu Jihad, undaunted, unaffected.

This is barbaric.

The Old Me pushes, nudges, tugs at my head, trying to turn me towards Liam.

You have to do something. Isn't that why you came here in the first place?

I work up the courage to look at Liam. His upper lip is trembling. He is biting his lower one. I look away.

Coward.

It's not that I don't care. I want to comfort him. Tell him it will be okay and we will see our parents again, one day. Our countries will let us back in. Not try us for treason. Understand that we had mistaken virtual worlds for real ones. They'll see. They'll understand. They'll know what to do.

You need to get out of here.

The Old Me is already there. Rubbing his back and telling him what to do when he reaches town. Whom to call and how to escape...

Just then, a bump in the road sends our baskets flying. A baby bag hits the back of Abu Jihad's head. Instinctively, he grabs it like the head of an assailant and shoots its side as if he were cramming his pistol inside someone's mouth. Screams erupt as the bag explodes. Baby bottles, wipes and shreds of cotton hit the low ceiling of the bus, then float back down. The driver continues to drive.

Get out. Now.

I hold my breath, the bullet still ringing in my ears. The loud bang has blocked out all noise and I feel as if the whole world has gone deaf. Soft feathery bits of scattered cotton float in the air like snowflakes in the sky. I think of home. I think of Christmas, a tradition we were not allowed to celebrate in my strict Muslim household, but one that continued to fill me with excitement. I think of Christmas mornings, running down to see if Santa had visited, finding the little present that my mother had hidden for me without telling Papa. I remember how I would hide it from him, secretly cherishing the thought that Santa loved me.

You were trying to please him, weren't you? You thought your father would approve.

The Old Me holds my hand as we walk through these memories. I think about how my father had hated that he couldn't move back home to Pakistan. How economics had put shackles around his legs. He wanted me to live in a better society. A purer one.

No father would want this for his child, you fool.

For a second, I feel my two conflicting selves blending into each other, the battle inside me finally resolving itself as I realize what I have to do.

It's now or never.

I look at Liam who is staring straight ahead, his face pale, mouth slightly open, his tongue frozen. Bits of white cotton are stuck to his face. He looks like a young old man. An exhausted one. The Old Me reaches out and tells him it's okay. She turns to me.

Don't think. Just do it.

I had heard all this before. On the Internet, when joining the ISIS's jihad in Syria had seemed like the right thing to do, then, too, a voice had told me I was doing the right thing. Why should I believe it now?

Come. Take my hand. I won't let you go.

This time, I was on the other side.

Come back to me. We can be whole again.

In that moment, I try to join her. I really do. But some instinct prevents me. I feel the hot sparks of Abu Jihad's silent rage as he darts his gaze crazily around, fingering his trigger, trying to find a way to ward off the humiliation from himself. He'd just shot a bag of nappies. The story could become a legend. A laughable legend. His gaze rests on Liam and he glocks his gun.

Stop.

The Old Me steps in between. She pushes him away and calls him a sissy. A bully. A coward.

I want to join her. I really do. But something stronger takes over. Abu Jihad's angry features twisted in rage and disgust glare down at me. 'What are you looking at, woman?' he growls at me. Whether it's fear or an instinct for self-preservation, I am not sure, but I find myself reaching out for one of the nappies that landed by our feet. I pick it up, even as I feel Abu Jihad's murderous eyes boring into my back.

I place it on Liam's lap, where a deep stain is spreading rapidly.

I feel Abu Jihad's tense thighs that had been pressing into mine loosen, then see a thunderous laugh escaping his purple lips. He puts his gun away and turns around to face the passengers. 'Brother Lucy wet his pants!' he shouts.

The bus melts with relief. Laughter, as loud as the gunshot, bounces off the cramped interiors. Little bits of fluff rise like smoke. Even the driver roars with laughter, pretending to wipe the seat with his dirty jalbiya.

And through all this, Liam shrinks into himself.

So this is it. This is the real you.

The Old Me shakes her head. Disgust drips from her eyes like fine silver teardrops as she floats out of the window.

I don't see much of her after that.

Malady of the Heart

Lifting the flap of her inky black burkha, Ami Jan held the phone close to her mouth. 'I am taking Zara to the doctor,' she told my husband. But I knew what kind of a practitioner she was taking me to. *Dava nahi, dua.* Prayer, not medicine, was her cure for all ails.

I knew my mother well.

Fixing her veil back into place after she hung up, she turned to me. 'Cover your head,' she ordered, before summoning our old help, Halima.

'Halima, you stay here,' Ami Jan told the old woman, 'and look after the child.'

I could see from the way Halima was fidgeting that she was in no mood to be left behind. Halima, with her wrinkled face and pointy ears that had drooped with age, had an expansive appetite for gossip, and a visit

---

An edited version of this story was first published in *Writers on Writing*, 2013.

to the hakim was a story worth telling in the servant quarters.

'I better come, Begum Sahiba. Only four days since Benazir's assassination, who knows how many more blasts...'

'Halima,' Ami Jan cut her off, 'the child.'

Not one to be discouraged easily, she argued, 'What will the child hear at the Hakim's that he hasn't heard already?'

Halima had a knack for saying the most inappropriate things at the most appropriate of times. She had my mother in a tight spot, for further discussion would have brought up things we would all much rather forget.

'It's no secret that Zara Bibi wants a divorce...'

'Halima!' Ami Jan's eyes were forbidding. I looked from her to Halima to my son, unsure whom she was trying to protect.

'I am coming along,' the old woman responded stubbornly. 'Oh yes, I am. Stop me if you will.' And she scrambled down the stairs ahead of us with speed that defied her old age.

'Come on, now!' we heard her shout to the driver, thumping the car's bonnet, 'get moving, get the car ready.' Gul Khan, who could usually be found leaning against the car door, twirling his waistband, seemed unperturbed, for no sound emerged from him.

'If only she hadn't been with us for so long,' Ami Jan sighed as she led me down. 'I suppose we will have to take the child with us.'

I didn't protest. My mouth felt numb as if I'd been sucking an ice-cube and my limbs felt loose, as if I'd been soaking in a hot bath too long.

The child had been crouching in the stairwell, clutching the toy airplane his father had brought him a year ago. Hearing his name, he ran down the steps two at a time, his skinny legs in shorts making him look like a stick figure from a child's drawing. He held on to my leg and asked, 'I can come?'

I nodded mildly, the effort seeming Herculean.

'Mummy, mummy, where are we going?'

I stared irritably at him. *Why do children ask so many questions*, I thought. *I never did.* The child seemed to sense my mood and grew quiet, focussing on the windshield and the numerous decorations hanging from the rear-view mirror.

'Now remember, Gul Khan,' Halima began her instructions to the driver, 'there is a child with us, so no more of your rough, rogue driving.'

Then, turning to us, as if the driver was not present, she said, 'I swear, Zara Bibi, the man drives likes a thief escaping from the police ... which is probably what he was before.'

Gul Khan seethed but did not reply. Instead, he took his revenge by driving so slowly that pedestrians overtook us, and donkey carts and vendors went past. But there was something therapeutic about navigating this hurtling city so slowly. What was disturbing was the normalcy of it all. I was surprised to see how quickly life had returned to normal even though it had hardly been four days since Benazir's murder. *Perhaps,* I thought closing my eyes, *in death, all women became equal.*

When I opened my eyes, we were still far behind my most optimistic projection. My mother sat statue-still, covered from head to toe in her black burkha, while Halima, in her dirty white chadder, sat in the front, pointing things out to the child.

Summoning all my strength, I leaned forward and asked in a slow, drugged voice, 'Why are you driving so slowly?'

'Ask her, Zara Bibi,' the driver pointed his chubby thumb at Halima, who was staring out of the window. 'People who've never sat in a car,' he snorted, 'how would they know how it's supposed to be driven?'

Completely missing the sarcasm, Halima dismissed him with a wave of her hand, 'Carry on, you will learn eventually.'

Gul Khan's milky white complexion took on a purple hue and he looked like a character in a cartoon, about to explode. He braked suddenly, causing Halima to bump her head against the windscreen.

'Don't practise your driving on us, you—' Halima started shouting, but Ami Jan cut her off.

'Enough, Halima,' Ami Jan interjected. 'Gul Khan, just get us there.'

I didn't blame Gul Khan for stepping on the gas after that. We sped through the lanes of Karachi, scaring cows, running lights, ignoring shrill whistles of the traffic policeman, till finally we reached our destination: Hakim Dilbar's Dawakhana.

The sign, an immaculate square of white, stood out from the rest of the dilapidated building. I read it slowly: Bismillah Ur Rahman Ur Rahim; Enter in the name of God. I walked to the side where there was a tiny nondescript door with another sign above it, a cloth banner, like a tiny flag with black Urdu calligraphy. The letters, curvy and sensuous like waves in an ocean, read: Hakim Dilbar, Mahir-i-nafsiyat aur dil; Experts in problems of the mind and the heart. Practitioner since the court of Nawab Siraj-ud Daulah, the last of the great Mughal kings.

I turned around to realize that none of the others were behind me.

They stood a little way off, distracted by a vendor selling mud toys on a cart.

'Matti kay khiloney! Unbreakable mud toys, try it, buy it, try it, buy it, mud toys!'

Even in the distance, I could see the child's small face light up at the sound of the man's lonesome, weary call. He reminded me of myself.

'Mummy,' he called out to me, 'Mummy, can I have some?'

Just for a second, I felt my heart thawing.

But then Halima's shrill voice rose up, cutting into me like a saw. 'Hai! You can have the entire cart, my little Baba,' I heard her say. 'Just you wait here and I'll get them for you.'

'No! I want to choose myself,' the child argued.

'Come, then. But don't show any excitement. You don't know these rascals. The minute you like something, they double the price. Now listen, whichever one you like, say, "Ugh, that one is the worst," understand?'

The child nodded, though I could see he didn't.

The vendor approached, his nasal voice creating a melancholic atmosphere as he pitched his wares with the sadness of two lovers forced apart. 'Ah, look at this kettle, once a beautiful kettle, still a beautiful kettle, look at its cup, unbreakable mud cup...'

The child squealed as he saw the mud animals. 'That one! I want that one!'

The vendor allowed himself the slightest of smiles and promptly said, 'Oh little Baba, you have the taste of a prince. That one is the most exquisite.' He quickly placed the toy in the child's hands, 'Just one red note it costs.'

'Oho,' Hailma jumped in, 'do you think I was born yesterday?'

Gul Khan didn't help when he muttered, 'I don't even think you were born in this century.'

Halima ignored his remark and addressed the vendor: 'Don't try to fool us with exquisite craftsmanship, partnership, whatever. Quote the right price or take your sweaty face and roam the streets of Karachi for the rest of the afternoon. Arrey, who plays with mud toys nowadays anyway? As it is our little Baba has toys that can fly, talk, walk – even a little dog that does backflips. Have you even seen such a thing in your dreams, you miserable mud-toy–seller? One red rupee my foot!'

The vendor who wore a dark brown shalwar kameez stained with huge patches of sweat, shifted his yellow turban and I felt a surge of anger at Halima for bargaining him down.

The man frowned and said, 'Look at the workmanship, Bibi. It takes my wife six hours to make a single toy.'

'Take it or leave it,' Halima replied, 'we'll give you ten rupees.'

The man scowled at her. He reached out to take the toy away and the child shrank back. Halima, offended by the man's behaviour, smacked his hand with her Chinese fan.

'Acha, tell us a reasonable price.'

'The price is reasonable,' the man sulked.

My patience was wearing thin and if I'd had any money on me at all, I would have ended their little drama right there. For once, Ami Jan and I were in agreement. She managed to pull out a few notes without lifting her burkha and handed them to the toy seller. I wondered how Ami Jan saw through the gauze mesh that covered her eyes.

'Enough,' she held up her hand before Halima could argue. 'Now let's go inside,' she said firmly, marching towards the hakim's clinic.

Inside, a wall portioned the room in two neat halves.

Halima, Ami Jan and I were led towards one side of the waiting hall while Gul Khan and the child were told to wait outside.

'Oh, but he's not a man, he's a child,' Halima exclaimed. 'He is just four years old. Why can't we bring him into the women's quarters?'

'You can't,' proclaimed the receptionist, a fat woman whose flesh spilled off the steel stool she sat on. She smoothed the silky hijab through which her henna-stained hair peeped out; then, spitting a thin red arc of chewed betel nut juice into the spittoon, said, 'Even a pregnant woman is not allowed here in the zenana half, lest she be carrying a male and he may stain the purity of their purdah. This is a strict hijab-observing zone. Doctor Sahib's faith is very pure and, who knows, perhaps it's this strictness of observances that has bestowed upon him such powers of healing.'

I could see that Ami Jan was suitably impressed as she lifted the flap of her burkha and relaxed on the hard wooden bench as if it were a velvet love seat. But Halima continued arguing, 'What hijab zone? Never in my life have I heard...'

Seeing the woman's mounting irritation, Ami Jan decided to send the child home.

'Take him home,' she instructed the driver. 'Stay with him till we get back.'

'But he's only a child. Will it be safe to send him alone?' My concerns went unheard as I was ushered into the waiting room with just one sentence: 'Don't worry, he's a boy.'

And so we sat, till finally we got an audience with the healer. *The fixer-upper of Muslim women gone awry*, the sign should have read, in my opinion. But then my opinion didn't matter. It never had.

❂

Hakim Dilbar was a delicate man. There is no other word to describe his fragility. Nearing ninety, he sat cross-legged on a divan, mystically serene, untouched by the stifling Karachi heat. He wore a snow-white kurta pyjama that seemed to have been woven from the softest of threads. His white beard, white hair and unusually pallid eyes contrasted with the darkness of his pupils, giving him an ethereal appearance. If it weren't for the red rose in his buttonhole and the strong smell of ittar, I would have dismissed him as an apparition.

Ami Jan pushed me down on the silver metal stool while she sat on the chair nearby. Halima squatted on the floor beside the hakim sahib's throne and began her lamentations: 'Ay, Hakim Sahib, five years ago, Zara Bibi got married and went to Lon-don. Ever since she returned, she is not the same. Doesn't eat, doesn't sleep ... Arrey, she hardly even talks.'

'Halima, please,' Ami Jan shouted.

Just then, a rumbling voice sounded as someone cleared their throat. It was then that we noticed the other man. While the elder hakim sat on the throne-like divan, looking like a king observing his court, his son – a younger version of the hakim except for the lab coat and spectacles – sat hunched in a corner on a small white desk, behind a large open register and a row of glass bottles filled with tiny pills and forbidding-looking herbs.

'Name?' he asked without looking up at us.

We were too taken aback by the second man's presence to answer right away. Now the elder hakim spoke, in a voice that seemed to have been dipped in a mixture of sugar and honey and woven like a basket of banana leaves: 'He means which one of you is the patient?'

For some reason, the question made me smile. The smile spread further, erupting into laughter. Where had I heard that mad people always thought it was the world around them that had become insane? Looking at Ami Jan's alarmed face as I laughed, I could see that she thought I was the one who needed help.

'Nafas,' said the elder hakim, asking for my wrist. While the younger version pottered about with stethoscopes and charts, the elder calmly leaned back and, taking my pulse with his thumb and forefinger, closed his eyes.

When he opened them again, I stared at him and asked, 'What can you tell by checking my pulse that he can't with all his instruments?'

Ami Jan hushed me at my impertinence, but the elder man just smiled. 'Sometimes,' he said, scanning my face, 'the stream of our pulse carries the illness into those dark forgotten corners of our bodies where the doctor's tool cannot reach.'

I shifted in my stool.

'Come here, beti,' he leaned forward.

'Ijaazat hai?' he turned to my mother for permission.

'Proceed,' she replied.

I had heard tales of how some of these spiritual healers beat out spirits from the body, how the patient's skin was burnt to release a trapped ghost, and how they tore out your nails to remove the lurking evil inside your fingers. I shivered at the thought of what they would do to someone like me, someone so far removed from the realities of everyday life.

He held my face close to his. So close that I was breathing his breath. Before I could open my mouth to protest, he flicked my eyelid inside out.

'No!' I screamed, not so much from the pain but from the unexpectedness of it all.

'Hmm,' he mumbled. 'The secret thrives … it hides … in the dark.'

'What is it, Hakim Sahib?' Ami asked, clasping her chest.

'What do you mean? They haven't even asked us *why* we are here,' I said.

'It is,' he said, looking directly into my eyes, 'a malady of the heart.'

'A malady of the heart?' repeated Ami Jan.

'A malady of the heart!' echoed Halima.

'A malady of the heart,' said the son firmly, closing the register as if admitting failure and putting away his charts and vials. When we recovered from the echoes, Ami Jan asked, 'Surely, Hakim Sahib, with your powers, there must be a cure?'

Hakim Sahib ran his fingers through his long white beard and began fingering his beads. When he spoke, his voice was low and measured. 'The heart is the main connector of the body. It is through the heart that our body pumps blood, our spirit becomes purified. And it is through the heart that our desires become tainted.' He looked sharply at me: 'The heart is vital, but not supreme. We must remember we control it and not the other way around. The heart that does not listen becomes a danger to the self.'

As if in protest, my heart began to beat loudly against my chest. Thump, thump, thump. I felt as if I were standing naked – breasts exposed, nipples ripped out, only an unsightly, unruly bloodstained organ thumping itself into a slow, hollow, relentless beat.

How much does he know? I found myself thinking for the second time that day.

The sun seemed harsh and unforgiving after the soft haze of the clinic. I blinked and rolled my eyes, wanting to ensure that my lids still worked, despite being turned inside-out. Through the corner of my eyes, I saw the alarmed look on Ami Jan's face and felt a softening of my sickly heart. I was all she had. Me and her God. And Halima, perhaps.

We stood side by side, the three of us – silent, stoic and sad. Three comically sad women with ill-behaved hearts that refused to listen. Ami Jan, Halima and I – failures at the game of love. What must we look like to passers-by, I wondered. Lost wanderers searching for an address, newly discharged patients, possessed women hoping to be cured by the healer, the evil witches of *Macbeth*, or perhaps just three ordinary women waiting for a rickshaw. The thought was amusing and I began to laugh. But perhaps combining the laughter with an eye roll was not such a good idea, for Ami Jan began to sniffle into her burkha. She blew her nose with the flap of her burkha, and any sympathy I had felt for her disappeared instantly.

I rested my forehead against the cool trunk of a thick, leafless tree littered with advertisements. Wrapping my arms around it, I began to read the posters plastered on its trunk.

'Do you think you are going mad?' I read out. 'Think you are going to die? Get rid of the evil eye, come to Baba Ji, come today, don't be shy.' 'Has your manhood let you down? Contact Hakim Hikmat, sole distributor of the German Mr Lover Bombastic syrup.' I read slowly, my tongue feeling foreign around the Urdu script I hadn't read for eleven years. 'Are you no longer in control? Contact Sayana Buddhu, expert in Bangal Ka Jaadu.' And then, beneath the drawing of a heart split in two, there was a number and an address: 'For the Broken-hearted. You break it, we mend it,' read the slogan that ran all around the trunk in three tiers of tattered white paper.

A sniffling Ami Jan trailed after me as I circled the tree, reading the series of advertisements as if unwinding a string.

'Halima,' Ami said, 'stop a taxi. No use waiting around at an unsafe time like this.' I was unsure if she meant the city or me.

'Alright, Begum Sahiba. But taxi drivers are all thieves.'

'Oof!' Ami Jan replied, pressing her temples with her forefinger and thumb.

Just then, a yellow cab rounded the corner and I flagged it down, wanting to be of some use to them but Halima barged ahead of me. 'How much to Society?'

The man rolled up his window and left.

'Halima,' Ami Jan screeched, raising her voice to the loudest I had heard in a long time, 'have you gone completely mad? How can you bargain at a time like this? Do you know how dangerous it is for women to be out alone at a time like this?'

Halima bowed her head sheepishly.

Ami Jan turned away from her and bumped smack into me. Instinctively, we moved away from each other. But then Ami Jan suddenly looked me straight in the eye and said, 'Twenty-five years.'

She cupped my face and, though I could not make out her expression behind the veil, I could feel the grip of her fingers as she pressed them firmly around my face.

'Twenty-five years have I been married to your father. Never thought of leaving. Not even the times when *he* left me.'

I struggled to look away, but she held firm. 'He always came back. Men always do.'

Finally, I yanked her hands away. 'And what if it's the woman who wants to leave?' I asked.

Now it was Ami Jan's turn to look away. With the veil blocking her face, even if I tried, I could not see what she was seeing.

So I walked away. Standing a few feet away from the two old women, I surveyed my surroundings.

All around us, the city lay dug up and little hills of sand stood like miniature pyramids. Dug-up roads, abandoned pipes, broken electricity poles, half-constructed buildings – some pockmarked by bullet holes – made the city resemble a bombed-out war zone; yet, people walked about or stood listlessly like cattle, chewing toothpicks, picking their nostrils or twirling their moustaches. A few women stood at the junction which seemed like an unofficial bus stop. A queue of donkey carts, cars and bikes formed behind a bus that skidded to a sudden stop, blocking the mouth of the roundabout and causing angry shouts. A man wearing a dark shalwar suit, stained darker by the sweat patches on his back and chest, descended and slammed the side of the bus, as men quickly clambered inside and, when there was no more room left to squeeze in, they climbed on to the roof, squatting like stubborn monkeys. The few women wrapped their headscarves closer to their skulls and, with downcast eyes, got in next to the driver. Now the man slammed the side of the bus and shouted, 'Jannay dey, jannay dey, let's go, let's go!' running along with the bus as it picked up speed. 'Let's go,' he shouted one final time before clambering aboard just as the bus lurched forward, letting out a puff of smoke, its creaking body permanently tilted to the left and painted with colourful slogans and paintings of birds and planes.

I was so immersed in the whole rigmarole that I didn't notice Halima hailing an autorickshaw. The man stopped a few feet away and when Halima stubbornly refused to walk over, tapping her feet impatiently, he reversed, puffing smoke right into our faces. 'May your face be blackened if you lay an evil eye on me,' read the slogan on its back.

As we walked around to its front, I noticed several more: 'Look, but with love,' being the most prominent one, painted in bold red lettering, a pair of winking eyes drawn underneath. Inside, on the red patent flaps, a poster of the Punjabi film actress Saima had been glued patchily, her heavy cleavage spilling out of the too-tight blouse nearly accosting us as we struggled to clamber into the small vehicle. 'Once you come inside me, you'll never want to leave!' declared the sign placed right underneath the poster.

I could feel Ami Jan's horror as her glance fell upon the words. Halima, who was the last one to get in, unable to read, remained blissfully ignorant and chatted happily, 'Aren't you glad, Begum Sahiba, we didn't get into that looteray bank robber's taxi? After all, why pay so much for such a short distance? Rickshaws are a far better option!'

After twenty minutes of jostling against the steel pipes of the rickshaw and the impertinent breasts of Saima, I could no longer stand the rickshaw driver's smirk in the rear-view mirror. I turned to Ami Jan, but she sat so stiff and rigid that I wondered if she had turned to stone. 'Ami Jan,' I tried to speak over the roar of the rickshaw, but she remained stoically still. 'Disgraceful,' she muttered when we slowed down at a traffic jam. I thought she meant the rickshaw driver, but then she said, 'In our days, a woman left her father's house as a bride, and her husband's as a corpse.'

When I didn't reply, she took my hand in hers and said, 'Think of your child.'

'You want me to stay in a loveless marriage just like you did?'

'Oh, what is this love-shove? Living abroad has put all these ideas in your head. In the end, my child, love boils down to nothing. It is not love that holds a marriage together, but responsibility, property, children.'

All further conversation was drowned by the rickshaw driver turning on the badly tuned radio that blared out more static than music. Ami Jan and I stared at the back of the driver's head as he suddenly broke into a song. He upped the volume, impervious to the argument behind him. I turned to Halima, but she seemed suddenly subdued, tolerating the rickshaw driver's vulgar humming. I initially thought it was Ami Jan's harshness that had silenced her, but later figured it was the picture of the political leader Altaf Hussein on the windshield that had got her tongue. Altaf Bhai and I had something in common: we had both been banished to London and now wished to live there in self-exile. But, while I had ended up there through an arranged marriage, he had escaped a jail sentence. While I was powerless and isolated back in my city, Altaf Bhai still managed to wield the power of his sword over Karachi with ruthless cynicism and a deadly following. His supporters feared no one and, in turn, everyone feared them. I had heard that even the powerful were helpless against them and averted their eyes to the lootings and killings carried out by his henchmen.

When the rickshaw surprisingly stopped at a red light, a little boy selling newspapers flashed one in our face. 'Breaking news! Benazir's murderer spotted. Killer framed in full close-up. Breaking news, breaking news!'

I eagerly reached out for a copy, leaving Halima to haggle the price of the paper. I turned it over, searching frantically for a name, for a face; but all I saw was the silhouette of a nameless man, circled loosely. This blurry, hazy shadow was the killer. I let out a laugh, unsettling not only Ami Jan and Halima but also the rickshaw driver, who'd been driving with his head turned around to catch a glimpse of the paper.

'What does it say? Who killed her?' they chorused.

'This nameless blob,' I answered. As two heads bent over the page and one leaned over the divide, I pointed to the dark shadow of a man pulling a pistol so close to the back of Benazir's head, that if she had turned around at that instant, she would have bumped right into him.

The rest of the journey passed in silence. When we reached home, Halima's haggling was half-hearted and she let Ami Jan pay the full fare with lacklustre grumbling as she dragged herself inside. 'So expensive everything has become these days,' she mumbled. 'Prices are touching the sky.'

'Nothing is cheap in this country,' said the rickshaw driver, depositing the money into the folds of his shalwar.

'Except human life,' added the gardener, squatting by the gate. 'They'll kill you for a mobile phone down where I live.'

As I got out of the rickshaw, the driver asked me for the paper. 'Since you have read it,' he added. I was hesitant to part with it, finding some perverse comfort in having a real person associated with the politician's sudden death. *Life is precious*, it made me think. *Uncertain and short.*

Before I could respond, he grabbed it out of my hand, lingering for a second on my fingers. Gripping my wrist firmly, Ami Jan pulled me away from him.

'As if the first attempt on her life hadn't been enough,' we heard him mutter as he scanned the paper. 'And what good was her death to us? Complete shutdown for three whole days! Where is a day-wager to go? My four children and two wives starved for the three days I couldn't get any customers. All because of this Madam Democracy.'

The gardener came over and asked to see the paper. Satisfied, he nodded and said, 'What can you do, bhai? Women are impulsive creatures.'

'You are right, bhai,' said the rickshaw driver, revving up the motor, 'Women only listen to their hearts.'

That evening, the three of us sat in my childhood bedroom, underneath a still ceiling fan, waiting for the power to be restored. Ami Jan sat on the bed while I sat cross-legged on the cold marble floor as Halima oiled and braided my long hair.

'How dry your scalp is,' she lamented as she poured what felt like half the bottle onto my head. 'Do you remember how I used to massage oil into your head during your exams? Barely a childhood you had, with your nose always buried in a book,' Halima chatted as she rubbed oil into my scalp.

'Yes, how hard my daughter would study,' Ami Jan replied. She peeled an orange and passed it to me after rubbing it with salt and black pepper. 'From morning till noon, she would rock back and forth, repeating her lessons.'

'But what use? It's not like she has to go out and work,' Halima nodded dismissively.

Halima didn't know it, but she had just voiced something that had been bothering me since the day I got married. Many lonely nights when I saw my husband immersed in his work, I comforted myself with a magazine or a television rerun, trying to push away the thought that I too could have had a profession.

'An educated girl has better prospects of a proposal from a good family,' Ami Jan replied. 'See what a good man her husband is. She is lucky to be married to him.'

She stressed upon the last few words and I knew what Ami Jan was trying to tell me.

Another slice of orange was passed to me.

I remained silent.

Halima, as usual, did not know when to stop. 'But you are also educated, no, Begum Sahiba? And look at the husband you landed. Full of bad habits he was.'

I could tell she had gone too far, for Ami Jan put away the plate in her hands and turned her whole body towards her.

'It is the good fortune of a girl to have a caring, faithful husband,' she said. 'Not everyone,' she continued, waving her index finger at Halima, 'can be as lucky, but God has been kind to us. Perhaps in return for my pain, He has spared my daughter. Truly, it is a blessing to have a husband who is loyal.'

I knew the words would cut Ami Jan like ice, but I couldn't help myself as I said, 'And what if the wife is unfaithful?'

Ami Jan didn't talk to me for the rest of the afternoon. When we finally encountered each other in the bedroom, she was getting ready to say her prayers. I placed my hand on her arm. 'How long will you turn away from the truth, Ami Jan. How long?'

'Zara,' she replied, 'you didn't learn anything from my troubles, did you? All the pain I suffered, the betrayals, the humiliation...'

'But it was *your* decision to suffer. *You* chose to stay. Perhaps you did it because you wanted me to hate my father. Yes, you wanted me to hate him. You did, didn't you?'

Slowly, she raised her eyes to meet mine. 'I never wanted you to hate him, Zara. But I did want you to understand the meaning of loyalty.'

In the fading light, as Ami Jan sat on her prayer mat, framed against the window, she seemed only half the woman I used to know. I hardly recognized her, but then I hardly knew myself these days. All I knew was that I was no longer the Zara who grew up on a steady diet of fear. *Fear Allah. He is watching you. Fear the society – people will talk. Keep your mouth shut – even the walls have ears.*

'I want to leave my husband,' I said, silencing the voices in my head.

Hearing this, she folded one corner of her mat and came close to me. 'Zara, my child, your home is with him. You are lucky to have a husband who looks after you. He is caring, loyal, doesn't drink, doesn't smoke, doesn't beat you ... On what grounds do you want to leave him? Just like that? You got bored? Huh? That's it? Look at me. You cannot leave him. What will people say?'

'Stop, Ami Jan. Why don't you try to understand? I cannot live your life. I want to leave him. I want to be free. I am not the same person I was before I left Karachi. Please, I don't want to go back to my husband. I have changed—'

'You can't leave, my child,' she cut in. There was finality to her words as she opened the Quran.

'Ami Jan,' I tried again, 'I have felt something you never will. There is a world out there. Much larger. There is more to life than being a wife or a mother. I want to ... I want to live life on my own terms. Ami Jan ... please...'

And then I stopped. Tears were rolling down my cheeks.

'Don't do it, Zara,' she said. 'Don't break your marriage.'

Maybe, I thought as I looked into her eyes and nodded my head, my heart really was sick.

Now, as Ami Jan took a deep breath, it seemed as if she had inflated.

Towering over me, she began reciting, 'Qul auzu bin rabil nas ... Say, I seek refuge in the Lord of all mankind;

From the evil of that which whispers evil in the heart and slinks away...'

She was mouthing the prayer to dispel spirits. I bowed my head the way I used to when I was younger. For a moment, I felt the distance between us bridging. But then she turned and went back to her prayer mat. She was gone. Back to Him.

I watched her raise her palms to her shoulders and then fold them across her chest, touch her knees with her fingertips and then fall into prostration. She seemed to be falling and rising like a clockwork toy timed to perfection. Her lips kept moving all this while. Prayer after prayer. Praise after praise for a God who was never satiated.

Finally, she rested. Folding her legs beneath her, she raised her palms and begged His forgiveness. 'Tobah Astaghfar,' she chanted, sitting in an upright posture. 'Forgive my sins,' she repeated thirty-three times on each finger. 'Forgive me, Ya Allah, Tobah Astaghfar, God is great, Allah ho Akbar, The Merciful, All Knowing and Forgiving ...' her words making the sinking feeling in my stomach rise up like waves in my throat.

I knew then I would never be able to leave. My life would turn out just like my mother's. A wave of bile rose up my throat as I turned to her and said, 'Okay.'

✴

SIX MONTHS EARLIER

The day before I left London, I went to see Aidan at his home. Number 17 was a stoic black door in a nondescript brick building in a narrow dark alley. Bland and unobtrusive, almost as if it did not want to be found.

It was a small room in a small flat share. Everything was neatly packed away. A suitcase stood in the far corner as if ready to leave. Only a sweater flung over the chair gave any sign of habitation.

'So this is where you live?' I asked.

'For the time being,' he answered.

I nodded as if I understood, although I didn't. I couldn't imagine sharing a house with people who were not family. Ignoring the uneasiness, I asked him how his day had been, although what I really wanted to ask was if he'd keep in touch. I searched for answers in his eyes. *Will I see you again? How can you let me go? Ask me not to go. Tell me not to go. Will you ask me not to go? Will you? Won't you?* But eyes are not always easy to read.

We sat talking about a poem of his that had been shortlisted for a prize. He offered me tea. I declined. Silence followed as we stared awkwardly around the bare room. When it began to sink in that this is where it all ended, all I wanted to do was leave it all behind and just say goodbye.

'I have to go now,' I said when we had talked about everything other than what really mattered.

'Why so soon?' he asked.

'Why so soon?' and not 'Why do you have to go?'
I noted.

'I have to say my prayers,' I said, unsure whether
staying would help get an answer out of him.

'Say your prayers here.'

'Here?'

'Yeah. Here. Women don't need to go to a mosque,
right?'

'Right,' I repeated, wondering if he needed time to find
the right words or wanted one last fuck. The last thought
hurt so much, I felt like a thief who repents in the middle
of a theft. What was I doing here, in this strange room
with a stranger who lived in a house full of strangers?
What had I become? I felt metal flood my mouth and
all the tenderness I used to feel around Aidan began
to feel like a self-imposed lie. In the harsh light of day,
I felt cheap. An adultress, betraying her husband and
child who had done nothing to deserve this. Though the
windows were shut, I felt my senses flooded by the scent
of jasmine. Jasmine that came loose on my unfaithful
father's bed when he came home late, the fragrance
clinging to his body long after the golden goblet had
been drained and the women were no longer there.

I dropped to my knees in shame. Spreading my
shawl on his faded beige carpet, I began to pray without
performing an ablution. I raised my palms to my
shoulders, facing them outwards, I chanted 'Allah ho
Akbar' three times. I folded my arms across my chest
and recited the Surah Fatiha. I rose in ruku, kneeled and
bowed in prostration, then dropped again, rising to my

knee, chanting, praying, hoping. I don't know when it was that I began to cry and when Aidan took me in his arms. Together we rose, together we fell, our knees bumping, lacking any grace as we said the afternoon namaz. I chanted in Arabic and he whispered back, 'I love you.' I kept my gaze fixed straight ahead as I continued praying through his kisses. 'Stay with me.' I kept chanting the Arabic verses as he took my clothes off, kneading my breasts and pressing his nose into my neck.

I remember watching a spider crawl on the wall, a ladybug nestled in the folds of a jacket that hung on a peg as a thousand unseeing eyes looked back. I remember that my cheeks felt warm against his. 'Tobah Astaghfar,' I had chanted like Ami Jan. 'Tobah Astaghfar,' I had said as we kneeled on all fours. 'Forgive me, God,' I had whispered when we stopped.

Before I left, I had traced my fingers across his closed lids.

'I will be back, I promise.'

I didn't know then, it would be the last time I saw him.

The Hijab and Her

Nasira was busy looking up scholarships to US grad schools when the annoying professor called out a question. 'Post-colonialism.' The fat American instructor pointed to the title on the PowerPoint slide and said with a nasal twang, 'Now, how many of you are familiar with your own history?' He peered over his reading glasses and Nasira felt his eyes rest on her. And more specifically on her headscarf. She knew she had no reason to believe she was being singled out, but by some strange instinct felt as if the professor were mocking her. And more specifically, her headscarf.

Nasira felt her neck stiffen and the muscles between her shoulder blades tense as the man glanced around the room. 'Nasira,' he called out. She looked up from her screen, almost relieved that the wait was over, but at the same time annoyed that he seemed to think she spoke for all Pakistani girls her age. And more specifically for her headscarf.

'We were colonized by the British, yes, I know that, Professor,' she mumbled, her scarf rustling as she nodded. 'We all know that.'

'Ah,' the fat professor said, as if catching a thief red-handed. 'But that's not what I am asking. I am asking, who are you? Where do you come from? And how does that shape the choices you make in your life?'

Nasira let out a long, slow breath as she settled down comfortably for a long sonorous lecture on how South Asian Muslims were confused people who had been Arabicized to their fingernails. Without realizing, she tugged at her headscarf and together, the scarf and her, settled down for a comfortable open-eyed snooze.

The whirring sound of the air conditioning was soothing, and the professor's voice like white noise. She listened to him drone on, at times marvelling at her own ability to zone out.

'Now, you people often say "the partition of Pakistan and India" but really, it was just the partition of India,' he said triumphantly. '*You* were all Indians just seventy years ago!'

'But, sir,' a thin, shrill voice shook her out of her stupor. She turned around to see Zia – the only other Pakistani boy in their class, and one who felt more than anyone else the need to prove his patriotism – raise his hand.

'But, sir, officially we call it Independence Day. 14 August is Independence Day, not Partition Day, sir.'

Not one to be called out, Nasira turned back to see the indignant professor turn a slight shade of pink as he cleared his throat to counter-argue, 'Ahh, but independence from what? How many of your parents and grandparents think it was independence from the British? Oh no, my dear friend, the rhetoric goes that an Islamic nation was carved out of an infidel one. And it is this rhetoric that I want you to question.'

Satisfied that there was no further argument coming from Zia, he went on, 'You see, boys and girls, I taught in Pakistan for three years and I can tell you this ...' he paused for effect and cast a slow glance around the room, resting slightly longer on Nasira, or so she felt, 'there are some people there who actually believe that Pakistan was marked out the day Mohammed bin Qasim set foot in Sindh!'

He chuckled at his own sorry joke, making Nasira steam with agitation. The skin around her temples felt tight and she leaned forward, 'But, sir, doesn't that just absolve colonialism of all blame? I mean, the Brits are the ones who started the whole Hindu–Muslim divide. How come there was no conflict before that? For centuries, Hindus and Muslims lived in harmony and then as soon as the White man came and started his divide and rule policy, India split in two, and then three.'

Nasira was conscious that her hijab made a bigger statement than her words. A voice in her head said, *You're hardly the most credible person in the classroom to be accusing the White man*, and so she paused.

Picking up on that slight hesitation, the professor leapt at her. 'And what do you think of the Mughals and Mongols who plundered the subcontinent before the western colonizers, Miss...'

She knew he knew her name well, and was only pretending to forget to make her feel small and unimportant. He waited, expecting her to say it. So she didn't. She sat there tight-lipped, her hijab feeling itchy and tight around her scalp.

By now, interest had perked up in the classroom. Other students were beginning to look away from their screens and towards her. Some of them stopped texting and put down their phones. A few even had faint smiles, as if settling down to witness a wrestling match.

Nasira took a deep breath. The professor touched his glasses. The two looked as if they were ready to battle each other. The rest of the class leaned forward.

But Nasira had had enough. Her humiliation was complete. And so she pulled out a gun and shot him. In her imagination.

Ha, she thought with a silent laugh. If only she could. In reality, the only thing she could shoot him was a dirty look. And so she swallowed, looked away, and pretended to examine her fingernails. The rhetoric was not new. Neither was it old. History had been moulded in other parts of the world too, but what annoyed her about her American professor in this large American college where she was an exchange student from Pakistan was that they continued to mould history till it was no longer recognizable. One only had to look around at the Wild West theme parks, the cowboys-and-Indians stories, the revering of Columbus as the discoverer, to know that this place had its own way of telling a story. History is always told by the victor ... now where had she read that?

That day, while the professor droned on, she decided she was not going to fight it. It was exhausting. Let them pit all the Muslims together, measure all fingers equally, for when it came down to it, what he thought really did not matter. Her actions only mattered in the eyes of Allah. Only He could judge her. She pulled her headscarf closer to her skin, sank a little lower in her seat and decided that she would get through. She would get through till she had to, and when she could no longer bear it, she would join those who knew how to put the arrogant bastards in their place.

Nasira tuned out the lecture and opened her laptop. The cursor hovered over the tabs for a few seconds as a fresh wave of loathing washed over her. And then, with a single click, she shut down the tab for US graduate school applications and opened a new one. ISIS, she searched.

Fifty Shades at Fifty

Premji came home to find Buddhi sitting cross-legged on his favourite armchair. It was a 1950s' Victorian, upholstered in purple velvet, and he had spent many an evening snuggled in its lap, his head resting on one arm, legs cradled over the other. Now, as he watched his wife sitting with her feet up, her cracked heels grating against the pristine plush of the velvet, he felt a violent shudder pass through his body. He clamped his mouth shut and clenched his fists to stop himself from tossing her out right away. Buddhi, as he sometimes affectionately – often annoyingly – called his grey-haired wife, was a good ten years younger than him, but had gone prematurely grey. Among her many habits that seemed to irritate him, the topmost was that she loved sprawling out on the furniture to read whenever Premji's mother was out of sight. They had been married thirty years; yet, this was one habit she had not grown out of. They had no offspring, but

Buddhi's childish habits, Premji thought, more than made up for the absence of children.

Now, as he stood there seething at the doorway, he noticed that Buddhi had not even registered his presence. She carried on unperturbed, engrossed in the paperback she was reading. He watched in disbelief as she stretched one leg out, hitched up her shalwar and scratched at her calf. *Like a stray*, Premji thought sourly. His resentment was beginning to build up at this unceremonious welcome and he wondered if he should shout out his arrival. Then he thought perhaps making his presence felt by slamming his weathered old leather briefcase hard on the floor would have more impact. But then, looking at its tattered edges and frayed condition, he thought better of it. As it was, they were a poor couple, reduced to eating burnt food since they could no longer afford a cook. Leaving her cooking on the stove far too long was another of Buddhi's talents. This too, Premji blamed on her books.

He decided to clear his throat. As soon as the noise erupted from his throat, he looked away so as not to seem desperate for attention.

His gaze fell on the cobwebs in the corner of the doorway and he shook his head, for he knew full well what would happen if he pointed these out to Buddhi – she would blame the spiders. 'These spiders too could not find another place!' she would lament. And then feeling sorry for them, would add, 'But they have been living here for so long now. They are like the Burmese and the Bangladeshis. We can't just throw them out now that they've been found out as illegal immigrants.'

He sighed. Her logic was out most of the time as it were, and now, with money so tight, it was even more useless to argue with her. He looked back to see if she had noticed him and was shocked to note that she was still engrossed in the dog-eared novel.

'Ahemmm,' he cleared his throat slightly louder and looked away again, this time reflecting on how cruel time had been to them, reducing them to this suffocating little flat where they were forced to take in lodgers. He sighed again, thinking it wasn't easy living with his bedridden, cranky mother in this tiny cramped flat at the edge of Parsi colony. Many of the richer Parsis had moved out to the more affluent suburbs of Karachi, but Premji could not afford such a folly. Not just financially but also because he felt that here they were safe, away from the city's ugly, corruptive culture. He rubbed his chest and swallowed, thinking of the urban youth he came across in his administrative job at the university and the kind of good-for-nothing things they got up to. *Not for the Parsi community all this nonsense, oh no,* he thought, shaking his head vigorously at no one in particular. The Parsis were a fine community with none of this newfangled nonsense the confused Karachiwallahs immersed themselves in.

Neither here nor there, he chuckled, thinking he would just have to shake Buddhi out of her reverie. His stomach growled and he marched forward.

But as soon as he came close to her, he paused in his tracks. His glance fell on an upside-down placard by his wife's foot.

'Apna khana khud garam karo,' it read in roman Urdu. Premji felt heat rising to his face and, if he could, he would have emitted smoke from his ears, so inflamed was he by the sight.

'What is the meaning of all this?' he thundered, making Buddhi fall off the chair in surprise. Her orange and parrot-green nightdress fluttered nervously as she scampered to her feet.

'What, what?' she squawked, flapping her arms about. Her eyes darted from side to side like a sparrow that had fallen out its nest. 'What happened?' she said, with the disorientation of someone who had just risen from deep slumber.

Feeling vindicated, Premji marched royally up to the placard and, with the sigh of a martyr going to his grave, said, 'This. What is this?'

'Oh this!' Buddhi let out a high-pitched cackle.

'Yes, yes, this!' Premji repeated, his smug expression replaced with a pained one. Warming his food himself was a preposterous suggestion. As if he didn't do enough work in office, he was now expected to work at home too!

'This is Hannah's.'

'Hannah's?' Premji's frown deepened.

Hannah was the daughter of their Parsi friends who had migrated to Canada. She had moved in with them as a paying guest while she waited for her paperwork to come through before she joined her family. She taught gender studies at a local college and in between she filled her time by doing little marches and protests that Premji had noticed she called feminism.

All those marches and protests are fine, he thought, *as long as she's helping the poor oppressed Muslim women. But why in God's name*, he rubbed his chin thoughtfully, *is she bringing these provocative signs into a Parsi household?*

He decided to ask Buddhi, bracing himself for anything but a straight answer.

'What for?' Premji enquired in his sing-song tone, his voice losing some of its edge as he saw Buddhi picking up the novel again.

'I asked what the sign is for.'

Buddhi reluctantly tore her gaze away from the paperback and said, 'Arrey baba, it's for protesting, what else!'

'But what are you protesting?' Premji hollered, his face taking on a strange red hue as if his breath supply had been cut off at the neck.

Slowly, deliberately, Buddhi put down her book. Then she turned to face Premji with the patience of one addressing a mentally challenged patient: 'The sign is to use in the Aurat march.'

Letting out a loud sigh, she returned to her novel. But before she could open it, Premji slammed his hand against his forehead and said, 'All I am asking is what does this sign have to do with any protest and why is it in my house?'

This time, Buddhi turned her whole body to face him. She put down her book, smoothed the folds of her nightdress and touched up the loose hair escaping her bun. Then, getting up with some difficulty, she came and stood close to Premji. When the tips of their noses were millimetres apart, she screamed, 'So grumpy old men heat their own food when they can see their women are busy reading!'

Premji felt as if a strong wind was trying to knock him down and it took all his might to stay standing. He could sense her mood darkening, and knew from experience it was not worth it.

'Acha, okay, okay,' he said with an air of dismissal. 'Anyway, all this happens in Muslim households, no? Our community is very enlightened. Men and women all equal. Not for us all this nonsense.' He sat down and peeled his socks inches from Buddhi's scrunched-up nose.

'What's for dinner?' he asked, throwing them on the floor.

Buddhi stared at him, hard.

Once Buddhi had heated his food and slammed it down in front of him, she settled in with the book again. Till now, Premji had been immersed in the 9 o'clock news. Now he suddenly noticed her presence.

'Are you not watching the Kamran Khan show?' he asked, looking at her curiously as she swung her good leg over the sofa's arm and began reading.

'What's there to watch?' Buddhi snorted without looking up from her book. 'Same doom and gloom, stale breaking news, this political scandal or that. If you ask me, all these talk shows are gossip shows. I'd much rather read my book.'

Now this was highly unusual. Premji couldn't help but peer closely at his wife. *Is she sick?* he wondered. *No*, he decided, *just preoccupied.* But what was this book that had engrossed her so completely, he wondered. He and Buddhi watched at least three talk shows in a row every night. It had to be something extremely interesting to draw her away from these current affairs programmes where they both joined in the bashing of the Sharif family.

Scratching his chin, he glanced at the cover of the book she was reading. It was not even in colour! What kind of a book had a black-and-white cover, like an old film? Now Premji was intrigued.

He turned the TV to mute and cleared his throat, 'You have eaten?'

Buddhi grunted.

Premji stared at the dirty dishes in front of him, wondering if he would have to clear up after himself.

'That damned book,' he muttered under his breath.

'What?' Buddhi raised an eyebrow without looking up from the page.

'Nothing. I was just asking where you got the book from.'

'It's Hannah's.'

A silent alarm went off in Premji's head.

Clearing his throat some more, he said, 'And what is it about?'

'You won't understand,' came the response.

Now Premji was offended.

'What do you mean?' he roared. 'BA Honours I have from Karachi University and you tell me I would not understand a paperback? I have read Tolstoy, Chekhov, Shakespeare! What the bloody do you mean? How complex can it be? What is this book that is so un-understandable, huh?'

'*Fifty Shades of Grey.*'

'It's a colouring book?'

'No,' Buddhi said slowly, keeping the book down again. 'It's about a Mr Grey and a girl.'

'And what is so complex about that?'

'Well,' Buddhi dropped her voice, 'he does things to her.'

'What kind of things?' he asked, a hint of excitement apparent in his voice.

'Bad things.'

'What?' Premji blinked.

'Very bad things. He ties her up, he spanks her, he...'

'Tauba!' Premji exclaimed in the Islamic way, then quickly added, 'Ahura Mazda.' Getting up from his chair, he cried, 'What kind of trash are you reading, Buddhi? I'm telling you, I won't have this kind of nonsense in my house. You know how I feel about—'

'Arrey, no,' Buddhi pushed him back into his chair. 'She likes it. She likes it when he ties her up or blindfolds her with his tie before tickling her privates with a feather and ...' the more Buddhi described the scenes from the book, the deeper Premji's disbelief grew.

For a good few seconds, Premji was shocked into silence. He was not sure if he was more surprised that such a book had been written in the English language or that his wife was reading it. And that too so casually while he sat eating, under Kamran Khan's watchful eyes.

Feeling as if the TV were watching him rather than the other way around, the first thing he did was to scramble for the remote. He clicked off the TV, sending Kamran Khan's wordless face into a spiral of darkness. Then he turned to the breaking news in his own household.

'But, Buddhi, but,' he spluttered and stammered, 'you ... should you be reading this kind of thing? I mean at your age ... I...'

He nearly fell off his chair when he heard what Buddhi said next. She looked squarely at his face, and with slow deliberate words, and a ferocious batting of lashes, said, 'Oh Premji, *I'm* not that old.'

Barely had he recovered from the shock when she added, 'And neither are you.'

Premji swallowed. This could only mean one thing. But it had been so long ... should he ... *could* he?

As if to answer his doubts, Buddhi flicked her hair, the way she used to when they were newly married. And then a sudden gust of wind made her blink, making Premji freeze and wonder if she had winked at him. That was it. He got up so abruptly that he knocked back his favourite chair.

'It's getting late,' he said gruffly. 'Put away the food. And get my constipation medicine out.'

And then, as if it was a premonition, a second gust of wind knocked the placard onto his feet.

'Ahh!' he hopped on one foot, screaming in pain. 'That ... that silly Hannah! Get up, get up right now. Throw that sign out of the house, trash that trashy novel. And ... and ...' his face went from red to purple as he searched for some fault to pick, 'and close that bloody window!'

❈

Buddhi stared after him with a stoic gaze. Slowly, she pulled her hair back into her usual untidy bun and, pressing her arthritic knee with her palm, she got up. She tossed the book onto the chair with a kind of force. Then, as if overcome with guilt, she picked it up again.

'I'm only fifty, after all,' she told herself. 'Even Rekha is older than me.' Then, humming '*In ankhon ki masti*' to herself, she picked up his dirty plate and started hobbling to the kitchen, her stiff knee making the progress slow and painful.

'Are you tidying up or trying to do the catwalk?' Premji called out bitterly.

Buddhi hummed even louder.

'You are not a heroine in some film, you know,' he said, then in the same breath he shouted, 'Where is the soap? Why is there no soap in the bathroom?'

Buddhi stopped humming and shouted back, 'Then go use Hannah's bathroom. Unlike us, she has enough money to buy soap, at least!'

Suitably chastised, Premji made his way to his lodger's room, tail tucked firmly between his legs.

Buddhi went back to her humming as she washed the dishes. That is until an earth-shattering scream sent her heart racing. Leaving the tap on, she rushed to the room as quickly as her painful knee would allow her. But when she reached the room, she saw her husband frozen, his stare fixed unblinkingly on Hannah's unmade bed.

'What is it?' she pleaded. 'Have you turned to stone?'

When he didn't answer, she asked, 'Did you spot a cockroach?'

He shook his head.

'A rat?'

Again, he shook his head in silence.

'A ghost?'

'Worse,' he shuddered.

As if the bones in his body had melted, he sat down heavily on the mattress.

His face was ashen as he looked up and said, 'Ya Khudai, what is happening to our younger generation?' He shook his head and flung his hands above his head. 'Buddhi, I was on my way to the toilet when my eyes fell on her bed and ... and ... you know what I saw in the covers? You know?'

He waited expectantly for her to ask what, but when she denied him the pleasure, he went on anyway. 'Arrey, Buddhi, I saw ... I saw ...' he paused, wondering if he should indeed expose Buddhi to such a thing. He suddenly felt protective towards his fifty-year-old wife who knew so little about the big bad world.

As if making the decision for him, she said, 'Acha, now whatever it was, it's gone. Now get up.'

And then, before he could say 'stop', Buddhi yanked the bedspread straight.

'No!' Premji yelled, but it was too late. The thing fell on the floor with a thud and began vibrating.

Red-faced, he looked away and mumbled, 'Ya Khudai, I didn't want you to know, but oh, this new generation … oh Buddhi!'

Buddhi looked at the long, narrow, tube-like rubber instrument writhing on the floor and, with some difficulty, bent over to scoop it up.

'Oh, *this* little thing!' she exclaimed with a chuckle.

Premji felt the world shake just a little. 'You,' he stared incredulously at her, 'you *know* what this is?'

Now it was Buddhi's turn to look surprised. 'Why? You don't know?' she asked.

He flared at this. She might as well have accused him of being impotent.

'Of course, I am knowing,' he shouted.

Buddhi, sensing the downward turn the conversation was taking, pressed a button on the offending piece of rubber and switched it off. Then she looked up, a mischievous glint in her eyes. 'You know I often borrow it to massage my neck. It is very good for relaxing myself.'

Premji felt as if nothing in this world would ever surprise him again. But, just as quickly, his disbelief was replaced by an angry panic.

'Buddhi, how could you!'

'Oh, I'll show you how,' she said, the calm of her voice in direct opposition to the panic in his.

He opened his mouth to stop her, but it was too late. She had turned it on and, as the instrument slithered, buzzing and vibrating in her hands, she raised it slowly towards her neck and rolled it up and down.

'Ahhh,' she moaned, 'this is the best neck massager I have ever come across. Not even our old maalish-wali's hands can do the magic this little fellow can.'

Premji felt himself shudder at the term 'little fellow', but felt relief flooding his being at the realization that his innocent old Buddhi didn't know what this thing was *really* meant for. He felt slightly heroic, as if he had saved her from a great evil.

'Here,' she said, breaking into his thoughts.

She held it up as if it were a prize and, for a second, Premji wondered if this was a proposition. Was it a way to bridge what they were both feeling but could not voice, for they simply did not know if what they were feeling was desire or sheer fear?

'Buddhi,' he said, his voice quivering, for watching her like this was stirring strange, long-forgotten emotions within him.

'Yes?' Buddhi tucked a stray strand of grey behind her ears. There was determination in her eyes, and Premji could feel the sweat gathering at the back of his neck. He was unsure if this paralyzing feeling was desire or simply fear. After all, it had been so long.

And then, in a last-minute overtake, fear got the best of desire.

He cleared his throat and announced, 'I'm going to bed.'

But to his dismay, Buddhi followed him to the bedroom. He wondered if perhaps he had misled her. But it was too late. And as he sat down on the bed, so did she.

Buddhi kicked off her slippers with a gusto that made him doubt she ever had an arthritic knee. She held the book in one hand and the vibrator in the other.

'Really,' he said, shaking his head, 'What will become of that Hannah!'

Buddhi's face took on a sour expression and she spat out the saunf she had been chewing. *Like a camel*, Premji thought.

'Today's generation is not prudish like ours,' she said in a bitter, harsh tone. Though she had been addressing the wall, Premji felt as if she had called out his manhood. At the same time, he felt a little pang of something close to pity for her. She had been married to him at just twenty and had never known life to be anything but this. Buddhi had spent most of her life caring for others. It was almost surprising to see her do something for herself.

Premji felt conflicted. He did not want to encourage such behaviour, but didn't want to appear prudish either.

As if reading his mind, Buddhi said, 'You know it is a great massager. Perhaps you should try it.'

Premji considered the proposal. Then, with the same sour expression that he wore when losing at bridge, he turned to switch off the lamp.

'No,' she said, 'let's leave it on.'

In all these years of marriage, Premji, for one, had never seen Buddhi naked. And he wasn't quite sure if he wanted to now.

Looking away, he picked up her book. *This must be some book.*

Gently, she took the book from him and started kneading his shoulders, rolling the vibrator up and down his near-bent spine.

Premji winced and she shushed him: 'Stay still, Mister Grey,' and it was all Premji could do to stop shuddering.

He forced himself to stay still as Buddhi's rough hands grazed his cheeks. *Maybe it would be okay*, he thought to himself, turning his face towards her in stiff, slow movements. A stifled fart made its way out, the explosion startling them both.

'Buddhi, my stomach ...' he apologized.

'Shush,' she scolded, 'there is nothing wrong with your stomach.'

'But Buddhi, at our age...'

'Oh Premji, you are shy as a new bride!'

The phrase brought to mind images of a young Buddhi in all her finery, packing for their honeymoon. Of course, it hadn't really been a honeymoon, as Ma had insisted on accompanying them, sleeping in the same room as them.

Both seemed to take a moment to contemplate the disaster their sex life had been, thanks to Premji's mother insisting they sleep in the same room as her to save on the AC bill.

As if on cue, they heard the shrill voice of Ma reverberate through the house. 'Where is my food,' they heard the old woman shriek.

At this, Premji took a deep breath and said, 'Buddhi, you forgot to feed my mum again?'

Buddhi threw down the vibrator with such effort that Premji felt the room shake. And then she said something so caustic that not even the bitterest of Buddhi's burnt rice could leave such an aftertaste in his mouth: 'And this is why we could never have children.'

He sat there, holding the vibrator in his hand, its incessant buzzing numbing his palm, as he looked at Buddhi's receding back, her stiff arthritic walk and her dishevelled grey bun disappearing into the dim kitchen light. Slowly, he too got up and, shuffling back to the sofa, sat down heavily. He had with him the book Buddhi had left on the bed.

He read till Buddhi had fed and cleaned his mum. Then, when she walked out with the bedpan, he got up and walked towards her with the book in his hand. Then he did something he had not done in a long time: he took the bed pan from her.

Buddhi stood there, holding the book he had given back to her. When he returned, Buddhi too did something she had not done in a long time. She reached out and hugged him, the vibrator as well as the book forgotten as the two huddled together. With her palm on his chest, Buddhi felt Premji's heartbeat slow down and he in turn massaged her stiff shoulders till he felt her muscles loosening. They didn't need adventure, they decided, as they lay down and turned off the lights. What they needed was intimacy.

Only in London

The rabbit-hole went straight on like a tunnel for some
way, and then dipped suddenly down, so suddenly
that Alice had not a moment to think about stopping
herself before she found herself falling down what
seemed to be a very deep well.

I close the book and step off the Tube at Tooting
Broadway. Outside the dimly lit station, grey clouds
eclipse the sun and, for a moment, the whole street is
engulfed in darkness. It's two o'clock in the afternoon,
but here in London, it is neither night nor day.

A squealing of tyres, the grinding chatter of mixed
tongues and the rabid odour of waste and pungent spices
surrounds me.

I haven't been here in ages.

First published in *London Magazine,* 2008.

On the pavement, a shopping trolley stands abandoned. Next to it stands a band of old young boys with flapping Rasputin beards and listless hands. Thin, frenzied children trail behind grim-faced women in dull black chadders, while a halal butcher leans against his counter, listening. Outside his shop, a Somali man is calling upon Allah to come down and teach the pound shop owner a lesson for overcharging. And above all this looms a Primark sign, shadowing the street with its big bold letters. The effect is chaotic.

I think of Karachi, the city I left behind.

I walk down the high street towards The MADINA Store. Someone has spray-painted the last three letters with black paint so that the shop front reads 'The MAD Store'. A large Warhol-type poster of a man in a chequered headscarf aiming a machine gun decorates the door. Right next to it is a banana-yellow poster of Uma Thurman's *Kill Bill*. 'And Blair and Bush too,' someone has added with a marker.

Inside, the shelves are crammed with every possible item. Rows of children's toys sit next to bras and wigs, painting supplies are stacked next to spices and, in the back, a large glass cabinet is stuffed with 'used' mobile phones. A SALE sign sits placidly amidst the bustling shelves.

Behind the counter are rows of Bollywood DVDS and eye-popping film posters. In one of them, Shahrukh Khan's heart-throb face is twisted with rage while a wide-eyed, almost naked heroine stares up at him.

In front of this display stands a bearded man, lazily chewing betel nut.

Like a desert camel, I think.

'Salaam.'

'Walaikum Salaam,' he answers.

'A five-pound calling card to Pakistan and a copy of the *New Asian Woman*.' Hesitantly I add, 'And a pack of Marlborough Lights.'

He grins, and I shift my weight from one foot to the other. Under his stare, my shirt seems too short and the jeans I am wearing feel too tight. I put on my jacket, though the shop is warm.

As he hands over the pack, he asks if I've seen the new Shahrukh Khan film.

'I've got a clean print. Not at all pirated ... and for you, only six pounds,' he smirks.

The six comes out as sex and I glance at the neon sign flashing above his head. 'BLUE films sold here', it reads. I wonder if he is trying to sell me some. I'm about to scold him with the classic desi rebuke of 'Don't you have any mother or sisters?' when I notice the small lettering underneath the BLUE: Bin Laden Undertakes Enemy.

'You can do that?'

He turns around to see what I'm talking about, and laughs. I see a flash of rotting teeth as he says, 'It's a free country. People can watch what they want. Yeah?'

I don't answer back.

'I wish they'd get the trial done,' she thought, 'and hand around the refreshments!' But there seemed to be no chance of this, so she began looking at everything about her, to pass away the time.

Outside, the smell of curries and kabobs is overpowering. I feel a mixture of nostalgia and nausea overcome me as my stomach lurches and I glance up the road to the Curry House & Takeaway. It's buzzing with lunchtime customers. White, Black, Indian and Pakistani all huddle together under its squat roof, savouring Britain's best recipe for harmony: chicken tikka masala.

Steam from the food has fogged up the windows and the people inside seem to be drifting in an other-worldly haze. As I get closer, through the glass, I see a bald Asian man bent over his plate. His face is close to the food, slurping the last of his curry like a cat. With deft fingers, he swipes the plate clean, then licks his fingertips and smacks his lips. Next to him, a white woman shifts in her chair. She is glancing nervously at her partner who's waiting at the counter to be served. In between the furtive glances, as if she were in a thief's den, she picks at her naan with her fork and knife while taking great, big swigs of water.

'No dogs allowed.' 'Hallal only.' 'Bestest Takeaway in Britain.' Garish stickers greet me at the door and a loud bell jangles my ears as I push open the door. The owner looks up from his till. He takes in my dark skin and tight jeans, and scowls at the cigarette in my hand. A waiter lets out a low whistle, while a brown man in a long, white

Arab dress glowers at me. I hold his gaze, even as sweat gathers in my palms. He continues to glare back and my defiance melts to a plea.

Am I the only one feeling this way?

In front of me stands a fat woman wearing a tight Punjabi suit, her head covered in a slippery scarf-like dupatta. On each side, a child clings desperately to her, while a baby is cradled on her arm. She is young enough to be my age, yet older than I could ever be.

Behind me stands another girl, also by herself. Probably a student. She is wearing jeans and sneakers. She pushes back her jacket hood to reveal a skull-tight hijab.

'Sister, it is your turn,' she says. I step forward in my high-heeled boots and clutching my jacket tightly around myself, order a biryani to go. Despite the protests from my hungry stomach, I do not feel brave enough to eat here alone.

The man taking my order takes in my accent and asks, 'Indian?'

Silently, I shake my head.

'Bangladeshi?'

I shake my head again.

'You don't have a British accent.' He looks up as he packs my food. Imposter, his gaze seems to say.

'I was born in Pakistan.'

'I see.'

He heaves a heavy sigh and slips in a flyer, not too discreetly, as he hands me my food. I step out in the cold sunshine and take great big gulps of air. My whole body smells of curry and the smell moves with me as I walk.

I come across a dustbin spewing empty cartons, old newspapers and broken beer bottles, and pull out the flyer from the paper bag. I already know what it will be about. I reach out to trash it, but my hand hovers over the bin. A voice rings in my ears. It is my mother's voice. Words laced with fading yellow edges trace the air around me and I think back to a time when, as a child, I played on the roof of our house in Karachi.

Ami is bending over me. Her chadder shadows her face, casting a dark glow between us. 'It is a sin to throw away Allah's name.'

In my head, I can see what would happen over the next few days. Having carefully folded the paper and tucked it in my pocket, I would look for flowing water to discard it in. This was the only honourable way to dispose of material with God's name on it, or so I had been taught: a belief I found hard to let go of, unlike others which I had shed in the first few years of my stay here.

'I'll think about hell when I get there,' I say, and reach out to bin the flyer. But some small beliefs are harder to let go of than others. I take a long drag on the dying cigarette and exhale slowly.

The paper still flutters in my hand.

She, Alice, was just saying to herself, 'If one only knew the right way to change...'

How long have I been standing here? The book I had brought along to read on the Tube feels heavy in my hands and I can feel the scents of Tooting sweeping into its pages. A white shopkeeper, often called a foreigner by locals in this neck of the woods, calls out, 'You lost, love?'

'Am I?' I blink back.

Perhaps thinking I didn't understand English, he asks again, slowly: 'Have you lost your way?'

I glance up the street to where a group of young boys are handing out pamphlets and calling out to the public to fight in Iraq and Syria.

'I'm not the one who's lost,' I reply.

The man spits on the sidewalk and mutters something about immigrants before returning to his pitch.

I walk towards the cries of 'Save Iraq'. Not a hint of Arab in them, I think, as I pass the boys.

'Sister, please make a donation for our Palestinian brothers,' says one.

He speaks with an East London accent and his sandy complexion, grizzly beard and prayer cap send chills down my spine. He is talking to me with his eyes to the ground.

I don't want to support a war that is not my own war, I think to myself. I don't want to see the bigger picture. I don't want to be responsible for the entire Muslim Ummah. I don't want to be the saviour. I want to stay aloof.

'No, thanks,' I say as I walk past without reaching into my purse. In a shop glass, I look at my reflection and think, *uninvolved*. I want to think of myself as me –

immigrant to the First World, holder of a newly printed British passport and then as a Muslim and much later as a woman.

But could I really?

Here in Tooting, surrounded by Punjabi and Urdu voices, the black hijabs, the aroma of curries, the cries of 'stop the war' mingling with the pungent call to prayer, I question myself.

I waver.

To steady myself, I clutch the inside left pocket of my coat. This is where I keep my new passport. I run my fingers over its smooth texture and feel a strange sense of abandonment. Like the flying carpet from the *Arabian Nights*, this magical booklet could take me wherever I want to go. I was far away from the poverty, the humiliation and the struggles of the old country. The fight for democracy wasn't my fight any more. The flies, the gutters, the overflowing stench of poverty was not my headache. Let the ones who got left behind fight the honour killings. I had other things to worry about. Like how to say house without the 'h'.

I feel a thrill race up my spine. It's laced with guilt. Above me, the grey sky hovers unsteadily. It runs into tall brick buildings and races above tunnels decorated with graffiti, litter and dead rats.

'Paki go home,' says a wall.

I look the other way and walk on. *I* am not a Paki. Not any more.

I hug the passport closer.

'Nor are we,' echo the grey faces of the Asian boys in hoods and baseball caps, leaning against the graffitied walls.

I shudder and walk on. Carefully folding the coarse paper of the flyer, I keep it next to the passport. *I can write 'British' on the forms now*, I think as my fingers caress the little booklet. I'm lost in my thoughts and miss the turn I am looking for. True, they still ask me, 'Where have you come from?' And their accent still baffles me, just as my pronunciation causes them to say 'pardon' again and again. I don't know how to eat a scone, don't care much for Marmite, or enjoy a game of footie. But I also don't care much for cooking aloo gobi, frying onions or following the latest score in cricket.

I retrace my steps to the high street and standing at the Broadway crossing, the intersection seems like a prophecy. East, West, Pakistan, Britain. Paki, Paki British, British Pakistani, British? Maybe that's why the kids on the university campus used to call themselves Muslims instead of choosing one or the other, or both, like me.

'Sailing in two boats, trying to be both,' my mother would have said. Curious, open, refusing to choose, I would like to think.

Why shouldn't I be both?

'Be what you would seem to be,' said the Duchess, 'or if you'd like it put more simply – never imagine yourself not to be otherwise than what it might appear to others that what you were or might have been was not otherwise than what you had been would have appeared to them to be otherwise.'

At the crossing, waiting for the green man to replace the red, I stub out the cigarette with my heel. A group of girls in black headscarves pass by. They look at me sideways and whisper. One of them turns back to smile. Envy or pity, I wonder.

A sudden gust of cold wind makes my skin shiver.

'The sun here has no warmth,' says a nearby shopkeeper. He is stroking his long thin beard. He seems to be talking to no one in particular, his creased face bearing that timeless quality of someone for whom time has ceased to be a measure. He could have been a young boy waiting for time to pass or an old man unaware that time had already passed him by.

There are many like him here, I think. Disillusioned shopkeepers who sit outside their shops on solitary stools, stroking their beards and calling out their wares by making hopeless small talk to passers-by. Unlike the busy bazaars of the old country, they don't shout out the prices here. The price will be based on the customer. A pound each for the poor and filthy asylum seekers. Pound fifty for the blacks, because of whom almost-whites like them have to suffer. 'No bargaining, only fixed price' for the infidel Indians. For the old masters of the game, the goras, who venture into the ghetto for the occasional curry, the price is irrelevant. But not so for the 'white trash' who are here to make life hell for the 'Paki'.

'They prowl the streets looking for a Paki to look them in the eye,' the lady at the threading parlour had told me. 'And that spells trouble. Later, you could bleat racism all you want, but can you bring your son back to life?'

I sense the shopkeeper's gaze on me and I'm reminded that there are also those of us who have forgotten their roots and committed the unforgivable sin of assimilation. For them, they have only contempt.

In this old man's eyes, I glimpse that unabashed pride in prejudice. I break away from his vacant gaze and cross the street. *He* will always be a stranger at home.

'Who am I then? Tell me that first, and then, if I like being that person, I'll come up; if not, I'll stay down here till I'm somebody else.'

My biryani is giving off a strong smell and I brace myself for the wrinkling of noses and shirking away that would follow me on the journey home. People would vacate the seat next to me on the Tube, move away from me at the bus stop, and glance suspiciously at the bag in my hand when I emerge from the underground. But before I leave the smells and colours of my childhood behind for the odourless grey landscape of my present, there is one more thing I have to do.

Mangoes. The reason I keep coming back to Tooting.

And here is a whole stage of mangoes, delicately placed at right angles to make a giant pyramid. 'Produce of Pakistan', declares a sign proudly placed on top. For a second, I feel a sliver of pride for belonging to a land that produces a thing of such joy. But before I can ponder more, a bony man pushes past me to ask the shopkeeper something. It is late September and, from his thin attire and Peshawari sandals, I can tell he is a new arrival: probably on a visit visa that will be stretched to three years in hiding. *Or maybe he'll claim asylum*, I think, looking at his needy eyes and pinched face. The papers have been full of him and his kind.

I take in his salty grey features, unaware as yet of the dark bitterness of the rat-infested basements that await him at the takeaway kitchens, once his money runs out.

In my mind, I map out his future. 'Three years,' I say to myself. It wouldn't take him more than three years to realize the streets here are not paved with gold. And then what will he do? There is no going back empty handed from this land.

As I wait for them to finish swapping scores, I think about how, when the bitterness sets in, the man will become vulnerable to the Brotherhood. Religion will be the only solace. *The eventual fundamentalist*, I think. Aloud, I say, 'A box of ten, and please hurry.'

The man, noticing me behind him, moves to one side.

'Ahh!' says the shopkeeper, weighing the mangoes on his ancient scale. 'Mangoes and cricket are two things that bring everybody together.'

'Only money brings people together,' says the hungry-looking man. His eyes cut across to me and he mumbles, 'You can get away with whatever you want when you've got money.'

'That is true,' agrees the owner. Like an oversized Buddha, he sits cross-legged on a stool. Surrounded by flies and fruit, he looks as if he belongs in some tropical jungle instead of this forgotten SW17 ghetto that doesn't even have the novelty value of a China Town or the East End.

His stubby fingers deftly pack the mangoes with straw and strips of paper inside a cardboard box while he talks without once looking up. 'When you have pounds in your pocket, a flat in Knightsbridge, no one will call you a Paki. No, jee, no! They will call you "sir". Good to have you with us, sir!'

His large belly jiggles as he laughs. Alone.

Slapping down a ten-pound note, I take the packet and make my way back to the Tube station. I've had enough of Tooting for one day.

The box of mangoes tucked firmly under one arm and clutching the bag of *biryan*i, my paperback and a large glossy magazine in the other, I step into the Tube heading north. Tooting disappears into a haze of darkness.

In the train, I gaze at the rainbow of faces around me. A shade darker here. A shade lighter there. Here in London, where it seems that every person is half-white, half-black, half-Indian, half-Southall and half-Chelsea, colour seems only skin deep.

Yet, we wear our pasts close to our skin.

The Tube rushes through the darkness. I lean back in my seat and flip through the magazine. Glancing back at me from the glossy pages are sleek, honey-skinned women with poker-straight black hair. They wear Asian clothes tailored to resemble western attire. One model wears a sari with a halter-neck top, while the other has on a tight-fitted blouse and straight pants. A scarf is loosely draped around her head. The caption says, 'Hybrid'.

I smile and think: *Mongrel.*

The Tube grinds to a stop and I step out of the sliding doors. But on the escalator going up towards the light, I can still feel Tooting on my skin. And it's not just the mangoes and biryani that make me feel this way.

Just at this moment Alice felt a very curious sensation, which puzzled her a good deal until she made out what it was: she was beginning to grow larger again, and she thought at first she would get up and leave the court; but on second thoughts she decided to remain where she was as long as there was room for her.

I'm being jostled along with the rush-hour crowd towards the ticket ends. The jabs are sharp, the cries of 'excuse me', loud and impatient. I feel unwanted.

Was I longing for home?

'I *am* home', I remind myself, but a voice persists: *Then why do you go looking for the smells and tastes you left behind?*

I step out into the cool night air and join the sea of commuters walking down Kings Road. The air here is different, almost scented. But still bleak. Prejudice, albeit of a different kind, still hangs in the air. I look around me and then at me in the glass of the million-dollar designer shop windows I pass.

I stop walking and look up. The sky is the same as back home, but something feels different.

London is not my city and never will be.

Alone in the crowd, I watch faces, perfectly still and expressionless, hands carrying Blackberries and Burberry, restless fingers typing away.

Because London is not even a city.

As people drift past me, I think, like a patchwork quilt, it is a series of countries within a city, bursting at the seams and held together by the sheer will of its people. Almost as if Tooting were a country with its invisible boundaries that contain the immigrant breeds, Chelsea is another such realm. It is a tight circle with limited access to those who could afford it. To live here, you have to be born into it or work very hard to get in. And even then, you can only look and not touch. You will always be the outsider.

By you, I mean me.

Later, as I board the Number 22 bus, a man in blue glances suspiciously at the packet in my hand and then at the cardboard box containing mangoes which takes up half the space on my seat. Ignoring the distrust in his light eyes, I focus instead on my book. He sniffs the air and pinches his nose.

I smell foreign and unfamiliar, even to myself.

Hunching my shoulders, I slouch deeper into my seat. The little booklet in my breast pocket is tight on my heart, but even its smooth caress is unable to soothe the unease I feel in that moment.

A boy boards the bus and sits down next to me in the tight space. He is dark enough to be black but light enough to be something else. He wears a white T-shirt with a black logo: Alien Nation.

'Alienation,' I read quickly.

Suddenly, I feel as if everything is illuminated. I find myself laughing. 'Isn't it ironic?' I say to the boy, who moves away to another seat.

I belong at neither end of this razor-edged city, yet I linger on like the stubborn smell of drying water after a storm. I think back to the icy cool faces of the boys in Tooting. 'Sister,' the boy had said to me. He saw me as one of them. I wonder if the police car that was parked opposite the road, silently witnessing the boys' petition, saw me as one of them too. I think back to the shopkeeper who thought I was a shameless imposter and then I see the man on the bus sniffing the air.

I close my eyes and think this is where I'll be when I open them again. At this very same spot from which there is no going back, but no way forward either. I no longer belong in a world wrecked by the fury of those who feel persecuted, nor do I fit in this new world, which has opened its doors to me but is indifferent to my existence.

What have I become?

'I wonder if I've been changed in the night? Let me think: was I the same when I got up this morning? I almost think I can remember feeling a little different.

But if I'm not the same, the next question is, who in the world am I? Ah, *that's* the great puzzle!'

The bus moves slowly in the gathering darkness, steady and serene, like the eye of a storm in the middle of great chaos. The lights dim at the High Street and I look out at the fishmonger who's just closing shop. I wonder how far the fish have travelled to be sold here. The fish stare back, their eyes cold, their mouths frozen in a surprised 'O'.

The bus halts at World's End estate and people at the back of the bus get off. There is a smattering of 'Oyes' and 'Innits', and boys with hoods and girls with tightly pulled-back hair and silver loops for earrings board the bus. A hooded figure with sallow skin and hollow eyes runs past me and up the stairs.

The driver hollers, 'You, boy!'

Nobody moves. He shouts again in a heavy Nigerian accent, 'Da bus not moving till I see yor teecket.'

We wait patiently till the boy comes down and mouthing a *Fuck off, Paki* at the driver, jumps off. A young Bangladeshi mother huddles close to her three children. A Chinese man closes his eyes. He reminds me of a cat.

The bus moves.

I look at the people around me. They remind me of the tiny pieces of a jigsaw puzzle that come together but never form a picture. People paused in a frame, as if waiting for someone to unclick them.

Hybrids or freaks?

The bus driver brakes roughly and a dog barks at me through the frosty glass pane.

'We come and go,' I whisper to myself and to the dog outside. Somewhere in the dark, a busker is strumming a guitar and a woman is singing.

'I'm like a bird ... I don't know where my home is...'

'Where my home is ...' I hum along.

I look out and notice the sky is lit up with stars, though it is not yet night. Amidst the twinkling of stars, a wane sun peers out from layers of thick white clouds.

Only in London can the sun and moon shine together.

I close my eyes and listen.

Only in London.

So she sat on, with closed eyes, and half believed herself in Wonderland, though she knew she had but to open them again, and all would change to dull reality.

(Excerpts from Lewis Carroll's *Alice in Wonderland*)

The Good Wife

The girl decides to wear the hijab against the will of her husband. She believes the hijab represents modesty, peace and submission to Allah. It keeps her grounded. It protects her, defines her. She cannot understand why he would not want her to. But he is no longer there to resist it. And these days she is free to do as she pleases. No one to stop her, no one to question her. Remind her. And no one to love her. But the good woman is brave. Courageous. These days, she has trained herself to wake up to precise images of normality. She wakes up, has breakfast, cleans the house, then spends the rest of the day on a prayer mat in her front room. She does not step out any more. To do so would be to give space to the horror outside.

Now, as the grey clouds gather on this heavy and pregnant London day, she sits all alone. Cloaked in

First published in *Trespass*, London, 2009.

midnight black, she browses through the leaves of an old journal and rummages through snapshots of the past, trying to find the answers to questions she doesn't understand. Each time, the sensation of his presence softens, but for now, she does not let him out of her head. She remembers him in seasons.

WINTER

That day, snow covered the city like a giant white blanket...

He came home to find her sitting on her prayer mat, chanting rhythmically, rocking back and forth, her eyes half closed and half open, as if in ecstasy. Her lips parted, releasing a few soundless syllables and then, running her palms over her face, she opened her eyes as if awakening from a deep dream. He sat down in front of her.

'When did you get back home?' she asked.

'I've been here for ages,' he said, lying down on her prayer mat. Her hand rose to her mouth as she said, 'Don't lie down here.' But he just smiled.

'It's so cold outside,' he said as he traced patterns on her cheek.

'Don't,' she whispered again, as if admonishing a naughty child. 'Get up,' she said.

And he got up, only to hug her tight.

'I haven't completed my prayers yet,' she protested.

'Your prayers can wait.'

'But the Almighty can't,' she replied.

'He doesn't have a choice,' he said and kissed her mouth.

STILL WINTER

A grey, watery, wintry day cascading gently into visions of Venus and Aramis measuring the price of hubris. 'Love,' says Venus, 'begins through discovery...'

The girl pours in the milk and then follows it with tea.

'The sign of an optimist,' muses the husband, who likes to prepare tea the other way around. Very lovingly, she stirs in the sugar, then hands it to him with such tenderness that a sigh escapes from the sparrow outside their window. The smell of buttered toast fills the air along with the inimitable aroma of home brew. Following her around the kitchen with his eyes, he says, 'I was thinking we should go out this weekend. See London proper.'

She smiles and he feels his heart contracting.

'You've been here, what, three months now? And I haven't really taken you out anywhere. Let me make it up to you today.'

'I'm ready when you are,' she says, and begins to reach for her headscarf.

He stiffens. 'You don't have to wear that if you don't want to,' he tries to sound casual but his voice is strained.

Her brow furrows in confusion. 'But I like wearing my hijab.'

'Yes, but I mean there is no obligation. This is London, you know. No one even has the time to look at one another.'

She looks up at him, her eyes puzzled. 'But,' she says, 'I don't wear this for *anyone*. I'm not hiding from anyone or anything.'

'Really? You *mean* that?' He is incredulous, for the man has spent a lifetime trying to blend in with his surroundings, his brown skin and Muslim name never allowing him the freedom to do so.

He pauses before he says, 'You ... you don't feel odd walking through the streets of London with people looking at you suspiciously? Like you're carrying a ton of explosives under your clothes?'

The woman laughs. Then realizing that he is not joking, she puts her teacup down and looks him in the eye.

'Look, husband, it's very simple, really. If people are going to measure all five fingers as equal, then that's their short-sightedness. I wear the hijab for myself, for my Allah. And I would not feel complete without it. It is second skin to me.'

There is a finality to her words and he decides not to say anything more for the moment. She too is silent, but her eyes speak. They are both on tender ground. It is one of those moments in a marriage when intimacy reaches unmanned peaks and couples are forced to confront the amount of their inner selves they wish to reveal to the other. The struggle begins between ego and desire. As their emotions fight it out in between the breakfast things, empty cups and half-eaten toasts, the husband reaches out and touches her chin. Desire enjoys a rare victory.

She fiddles with the lace edges of her scarf, tugging it further down her forehead.

He traces a finger around her cheekbones and says, 'All I'm saying, beautiful, is that you don't have to. I am not a typical Pakistani husband. I grew up here, in south London. I don't care if you bare your head or your legs or your belly. I'm not one of those men who get jealous every time another man looks at their wife.'

Again, she tugs the hijab back into place and says softly, 'But I care.'

He looks unconvinced. She presses further. 'Listen to me, husband. Please. My hijab is my identity. My calling card. I know who I am, where I come from and where my place is in the world. I know that sometimes it may make you feel uncomfortable with the way people view me suspiciously. No, no, don't deny it. And don't think I haven't noticed that people move away from me at the bus stop or change their seat when I sit down next to them. And I know you don't like women who wear the full veil. I've heard you call them blackbirds and crows and ninjas and all sorts.'

The woman looks so earnest that he has no choice but to listen as she says, 'Look, the only reason I socialize with them is because hardly anyone else in this neighbourhood talks to me. They either pity me as the poor repressed woman or fear me as a terrorist.'

The husband looks down at his feet, a surge of colour deepening the back of his neck. He seems unsettled by her sudden, unexpected outburst.

The woman stops speaking. She comes closer. Cupping his face in her palms, she tries to appeal to something deep inside him that she hopes is dormant and not dead. 'Listen, all this only strengthens my belief in my faith. You know that no one forced me. I *chose* to veil.'

He takes her hand in his own and draws her close. Pressing her hips into his body, he whispers, 'And I want to know why someone so beautiful wants to hide herself from the rest of the world.'

'Because Allah told me to.' She pushes his hand away and reaches out for a copy of the Quran. 'See here, it says so in Surah Nur, "And say to the believing women that they should lower their gaze and guard their modesty ... that they should draw their veils and not display their beauty."'

He shakes his head, 'Oh, come on.' He begins to walk away, but she grabs his hand.

'Don't walk away from me.'

He stops.

She walks around him and turns his face towards her own. 'Please try to understand,' she pleads. 'All through our wedding, my move to this new country, it is religion that has been my anchor. My faith keeps me grounded.'

'And me?'

There is a strange unfamiliar look in his eyes and for a second the woman feels as if needles are being pierced into her body. Needles sharpened with guilt and coloured with hubris. She knows she has hurt him.

She envelops him in her long black cloak and whispers, 'My devotion is for Allah, but all my passion is for you.'

'Prove it.'

'I will.'

SPRING

When the flowers found face again, spring scattered the air with tiny blossoms and the scent of love. People stopped throwing themselves on subway tracks, postmen started delivering lost mail, and the English started smiling, the husband and wife decided to visit the park.

The man and woman lie on the grass. Such peace surrounds them that passers-by are forced to stop and look at them. They are still. He in a brown suit that reflects his coffee-bean skin like an aura around him and she enveloped in a long, black garment, which makes her look like a mythical creature from afar. How long had they been lying there? Still and serene amidst the tiny pink daisies sprouting among the mustard green leaves of Hyde Park, they seem almost organic. A newborn's tranquillity reflects off their faces, as if they had been birthed right then and there in that very spot. They do not touch but seem to have an unbreakable connection.

'I could lie in your arms forever,' he whispers in her ears. The spell is broken. She smooths her scarf and laughs.

'I mean it,' he persists.

'What a thought, husband. You should find something more useful to do,' she teases him.

'I think... I really do. I think we have a connection. Whatever this bond is ... it makes me want to live ... forever.'

'The way you talk,' she laughs, 'you sound like some spoilt English public school boy. Who'd think you were a good ol' Muslim lad from south London.'

'Oye, watch it.' And he holds her close. Closer than the darkness that surrounds them as the sun sets and night ushers in all kinds of mystique.

SUMMER

The night is still and restless at once. The night is ironic. The night is significant. Tonight, a dream is being filled with bags of hope and make-believe, the kind that angels preach in faraway heaven when God makes a mistake. If only the meaning of events did not elude us as they unroll through our lives.

The bed stretches beneath them like sand. Desperate for some sparks of wisdom to prove his love, the husband whispers, 'I think I love you more than I love life. I want to live inside you.'

'Hush,' she places her palm against his mouth. She feels as if perfumed clouds have descended upon their dark airless house. He climbs upon her and, entering her, whispers, 'Let me make you my home.'

She pushes him off and straddles him between her knees. With her long dark hair covering her breasts, she looks like an ancient goddess. The goddess laughs.

'Like the tinkling of a thousand wine glasses. Like the gushing of a hundred fountains,' he muses as she moves above him.

When the pleasure has run through them, she turns to him and says solemnly, 'It is all His greatness, you know. He creates us and he instils this love inside our hearts. What you are feeling, my beloved husband, is Allah's magnitude.'

'I think what I'm feeling is love for my wife.'

'And I thank Him for putting that love in your heart.'

Their eyes lock and they gaze into a painted future until he suddenly turns his head away.

'What if one day I went away, wife? Would you miss me?'

She points her index finger upwards and says, 'There is no soul but has a protector over it.'[1]

'Is your faith really so strong, wife?'

'Strong enough to be able to withstand suspicious glances and funny remarks.'

'Sometimes I feel bad my family got you married to me and brought you to London, far away from your family in Pakistan. You must feel so awkward here.'

'No, I don't feel awkward. I don't know why you keep asking me that.'

He props himself up on one elbow and traces her chin with his index finger. 'You won't like this but ... why don't you just stop wearing your hijab?'

She turns away her face and he feels a river of remorse gush through his body.

---

[1] Surah 86. The Morning Star, The Nightcomer

'Are you ashamed of me?' she asks without looking at him.

He remains silent.

'I worry about you,' he says, his gaze elsewhere. 'That's all.'

'Well, let me tell you something.' Her voice is firm and controlled as she looks him in the eye. 'I'm not ashamed of my faith. My hijab is part of me. It's my Muslimness. It sort of announces my arrival. Anyway, why do you people in the West always think that hijab is a symbol of submission?'

'I don't know, maybe because it forces you to cover up?'

'And to bare herself is a woman's right?'

He stares at her before he begins to laugh.

Later, he asks her what she wants to do most in the world and she tells him she wants to travel the world. 'I promise,' he says. 'I promise I will take you, hijab and all,' he winks and she throws a pillow at him. It bursts into a rain of soft feathers and they are locked in a timeless moment. Across the feathers, they silently confess to each other a bond that no marriage union, whether arranged as theirs or through love and courtship, could have created. A bond of friendship.

AUTUMN

A season of grey, neither night nor day. It was that time of year when stones bled and birds fled to the south. A season of migration for some and for others, a season of betrayal.

When the tears finally come, they flow like a flood. She buries her nose in his shirt and tries to inhale his essence. 'Why did you leave me like this?' she keeps asking. In the same city as she, not too far away, a whole world lies burnt. Flesh and plastic mingling with steel as flames lick at every inch of their being. They tell her that her husband is dead. 'He that was born to the earth shall return one day to his Maker.' It is not his death she mourns but the fact that they suspect him as the suicide bomber.

She tries to tell them that he had gone to the US embassy for a visa. But they are only interested in knowing if he had visited Afghanistan, Pakistan, Syria, Iraq ... Did he know other terrorist networks ... Was he working alone or with someone? She concentrates on the blue of their uniform to block out her husband's absence. As if she were talking to a friend and not to the police, she says, 'We wanted to have children. We were going to start a family. The firstborn ... if it was a son, we were going to name him Mohammed. After the Prophet. And if it was a daughter, we'd call her Ayesha. We were going to have four children. We were ... so happy.'

She wipes a single tear from her cheek and looks at the man in blue. He is holding out some papers at her.

'You think he is the killer just because he was Muslim?'

The man stays silent, but in her head, she imagines him saying, 'You are an extremist. You dress like one. Your husband has to be the suicide bomber who killed himself, injuring many others, outside the US embassy.'

The good wife is loyal. From right to left and left to right, she shakes her head, as if possessed. 'No, sir, my husband wasn't suicidal; he was a very happy man. He told me himself that he loved me more than the world. He wanted to live forever.'

When the man says nothing, she starts beating her chest and shouting, 'No, sir, he wasn't an extremist or a terrorist. He was a good man. My husband was a good man. It was *my* faith that killed him. It was *my* love of God, for which he wanted to prove his worth. *I* killed him. *I* am the killer.'

'We won't get anything out of her today,' the man murmurs to his colleague. A woman with long and slender white fingers hands her a tissue.

Later, when she has stopped crying, they tell her they have intelligence that he was part of a sleeper cell. He was an Islamist.

'You are wrong,' she argues. 'He did not even want me to wear the hijab. He just wanted to be normal. To be accepted, like everyone else.'

Looks are exchanged before one of them says, 'Perhaps it was a front.'

'What do you mean?'

'He may have been using you. Perhaps he was an extremist masquerading as a moderate man. He was dangerous. We have information...'

She feels the world around her sway just a little before her head hits the ground.

WINTER ONCE AGAIN

The heavy curtain of rain strung with the white lace of fog bade the autumn goodbye, heralding the unstoppable change of seasons. Once again, darkness had prevailed. A season in between.

At the funeral, she wore her shroud in black. The veil still hung across her face and she fiddled with the edges. Women were not allowed into the graveyard, but they hadn't been able to stop her.

When the first fistful of soil was thrown into the grave, she cried, 'He is returning to his Maker.' The few present looked at her, astonished.

'Don't cry for him,' she said in between huge sobs that shook her entire body. 'Don't cry for him,' she kept saying as she stood by the mud grave where they buried a few of his teeth – the only parts of him that survived the blast.

She was the last one left.

The good wife now became the good widow. That was the last time she left her husband's house. 'Any time now,' she would repeat to herself, 'he'd return home and take me into his arms, prying me away from my prayers. Any time now.'

Coach Annie

At first I was a curiosity, a nuance, then a nuisance, an irritation, a problem and finally a thing of hate. They say when people start to hate you, it's because they are afraid of you. Afraid of your power. Well, I was getting plenty of hate. Did that make me powerful? I suppose so.

I'd always been the odd one out in our little Yorkshire town. The Paki girl with the headscarf and the spots. In that order, believe it or not. It should have been the other way around. The spots came first. Angry red dots that decorated my face like a Christmas tree. My mother made me scrape my oily skin with wire mesh and wash my face with hard soap, every day – but that only made it worse. My face became dry and scaly like the skin of a desert lizard. The eczema spread to my scalp and, slowly but surely, my hair began to fall off.

I was the only daughter amidst four sons, and my mother could not bear the shame. That's when the headscarf came into the picture. One day, she approached me with a beautiful pink cloth and wrapped it around my bald head, tucking the ends under my chin. The look of joy in her eyes was unforgettable. I too felt as if I had finally validated my femininity to her.

She made it out to be a religious thing, bragging to our neighbours about how devout her little girl was, and somewhere along the way, I began to believe it too. I took my hijab very seriously, even if not my prayers. I suppose, at that point, I just preferred the cloth to a wig. Believe me, wearing a wig is a bit of a challenge when you're just eight. Having a piece of cloth wrapped around my head was a lot easier than juggling a mop of hair when the biggest thrill in life was running senseless in the backyard with my brothers, mum shouting that we're the devil's lot. No one listened to her. Even back then.

Sometimes I wondered if she was invisible, for, despite her shrill voice, people had a habit of walking off while she was talking. And she loved to talk. Those days, it was about my hijab. She couldn't gloat enough about how we were all going to heaven thanks to her virtuous daughter, how proud she was of me for wearing the hijab and embracing God's will, of my big, big sacrifice. I usually stared blankly while she babbled away, wondering how slapping a piece of cloth on one's head could guarantee free entry into the pearly gates. And why she didn't wear one herself if it was, indeed, so special.

To be fair, she tried. But Mum couldn't bring herself to wear one regularly, though she covered her head loosely with a shawl when she stepped out. Too much trouble, she'd say, buying me beautiful silk scarves to tie around my head instead. But I preferred her tea cloths to the fancy embroidered ones she got for me from Bradford. I just couldn't handle the silky material she preferred. It skidded all over. The plain, coarse, skull-hugging hijab suited me. Snug and neat along my bony skull, slipping on like a balaclava, and staying there. It sure stopped our nosy Pakistani neighbours from speculating what sins my mother had committed for baldness to befall me.

I think we all assumed it would be a temporary thing. But my hair never grew back. Instead, the hijab grew on me. It became an extension of me. A part of me. It kept me grounded. Reminded me that God was watching out for me. I was no longer just the odd-looking girl with the wrong skin, wrong colour, wrong hair. Instead, I was *that* Muslim girl.

People left me alone. And believe me, it suited me just fine.

Did it get lonely? Yes, it did. But that was okay because I had four younger brothers to take up all my time. I was happy to play football in the yard with them when we weren't all fighting and trying to kill each other.

Fast forward to my teen years and I found myself being offered a government grant to go to university to study sports therapy. Part of the deal was that for six months prior, I had to work with the community youth with whatever task was assigned to me, be it teaching or coaching or care-giving. My only hesitation was that it meant getting out there and helping strangers. Usually troubled ones. It meant interaction. And I was scared. I was used to hiding away, melting into the scenery, avoiding socialization at all costs. Having an overprotective mother helped. My life was just school and home. I rarely went out. I couldn't ever remember talking to a stranger.

'This is your chance to get an education. Grab it,' my brothers told me and, not for the first time, I wondered why they were so different from my shy and reticent father whose world, like mine, was the factory and home. 'Give it a try,' my brothers urged. 'People would give an arm and a leg to get a full scholarship.'

So I went ahead and signed up, waiting for my first assignment.

I'd been tossing a ball around in the community centre one chilly January morning when one of the bosses stepped out, asking for a volunteer. I watched curiously as the suited man said in a high-pitched, anxious voice that he needed someone to coach a team. I should have known by the tremble in his voice that this was no little league. I offered myself, and the sacrificial cow that I was, the gods were satiated.

I still don't know if God was trying to help me or kill me. All I know is that he was testing me. First day on the pitch and I found myself trying to tell a bunch of towering Geordie lads with learning difficulties, that I was there to coach them. There was a fair bit of laughter and I saw myself through their eyes. A five feet two inches Asian girl with a headscarf. Not exactly cutting the stereotypical cult figure of a macho coach with a gut, slapping his thighs and yelling, 'Come on'.

The shock was mutual, for I had expected young boys, not six-feet–tall, gigantic lads with special needs. But while I hid my fear, they made their feelings crystal clear. They didn't say anything; no, those lads didn't. But on the pitch, the anger and the fury at being told what to do by a wee little lass in a hijab came out. They fell on me, kicked me, pushed me, roughed me up.

All part of the game. I can't complain.

Someone once told me that part of winning was showing up. So I showed up day in and day out. My bruises got deeper, my bones cracked some more, one swollen eye stopped opening all the way. I took it on the chin. Like a sport.

It became a kind of joke. But then I was used to jokes. On me, that is.

The joke is on me. Like my headscarf, it was part of me. *Chin up*, I'd tell myself and march out into the field, my mother yelling at me that I should forget uni-shuni and go see a doctor to get my head checked, and that I should get a normal job at the supermarket checkout like all the other Asian girls my age.

Sometimes, even my brothers winced when they saw my injuries.

'There are easier ways to kill yourself,' my younger brother said to me one day, as he carried me off the field after a particularly gruelling match. But I shook my head.

'I love sports,' I managed to say between the blood oozing from my mouth. 'I love the field.'

The attempts to accidently yank off the headscarf were many, though none was successful. I always wondered what they expected to find. The roughest guy in my team was the smallest lad on the pitch, and he was usually the one doing the headlocks. The biggest guy, his brother, usually went for my whistle. Gio and Sacha. They were simple guys with a black-and-white view of the world, sure that everything bad had to do with my kind. So sure that sometimes even my own faith shook.

It was around then that 7/7 happened. I went home and cried my lashless eyes out. It seemed so senseless. But I guess violence made the world go around. It was like night and day, I often thought. Where there is love, there is hate. And if hate is power, then perhaps this was a struggle between the love of power and the power of love.

I would soon find out.

Six weeks down, I was nearly done with my coaching credits when a player tripped me. I broke my ankle. Sadly, it didn't break my spirit. I showed up, crutch and all. Faith can make you do a lot of illogical things, but sometimes it can also give you the strength to push ahead.

I showed up, ready for more abuse. But something changed that day.

'Man, Annie, there ain't no stopping you, is there?' One of the players said, cracking a smile.

I shook my head. Truth was, I didn't know any better. There was nothing else out there for me. Off the field, I was the bald, eczema-ridden, Muslim fundo. On the field, I was fire. It fired me up, football.

'Why don't you play professional?' the same player asked me later that day.

I smiled and pointed to my headscarf. 'They don't allow professional footballers to wear a hijab.'

He tugged at it playfully. 'It can't mean that much to you. Not worth giving up your dream.'

My heart did a little jump and I stepped back. This little tug felt more brutal that all the shoves and kicks the lads had landed. I realized then that my hijab did mean something to me. It wasn't just a cover to hide my scanty hairline. It defined me, it was part of me.

That night, I stood in front of the mirror without my hijab. I wore a baseball cap on my head. 'Go Arsenal,' I shouted. The person in the mirror mimicked me. I didn't know who she was.

Last day of coaching, I had a surprise waiting for me. I had been offered a paid position that I could take up along with college.

I was sure the team would make a fuss, but the biggest shock was that I found out that the lads wanted me to stay on. Somehow, something had changed. I had been accepted. These big strong lads who struggled with reading and writing had understood something I could never have expressed in words. Gathering around me in a circle, they told me to 'go on and take it'.

And I did. To this day, I'm not sure if it was my coaching that made them change their minds or my stubbornness. But, just like that, everything changed.

Something healed inside me that day. It was as if all the broken bones had joined together and the scrapes and cuts had healed. As if someone had placed a cold press on a bruise. Later that week, six new lads went on to join the team and I braced myself for a repeat. But the first day the mocking came, it was none other than Sacha and Gio who stood up for me and said, 'Leave her alone. She's alright, our Coach Annie is.'

Needless to say, it set the tone.

I found myself looking in the mirror again that night. My skull-tight black hijab almost blending into my dark skin scarred with small cuts and scarlet-hued bruises. This time, I recognized the girl in the mirror for who she really was. And it was a relief. I felt easy. My joints felt loose. I was no longer the spotty Muslim girl in a headscarf.

Instead, I was *Coach* Annie.

Acknowledgements

A Series of Untimely Thank-yous:

Thank you to Kanishka Gupta for pushing me to write this book, and to the wonderful Udayan and Prema at HarperCollins for bringing it to the bookshelves with their constant support and help.

Heartfelt thanks to my lifelines – Naheed, Nimra, Najia, Sohema, Zeenia, Perviz and Eiman – friends who kept me afloat during the stormy tide that my life can be.

A shout-out to my brilliant students at Habib University who constantly fuel my imagination and provide food for thought.

But above all, a huge thanks to my husband Shahzeb and our lovely children Danyal and Selina Maya, without whom this book would have been written much sooner but would not have been half as interesting! Thank you for being in my life and for the drama, the tears and the hugs that make it so, so worth it.

Shukriya, also, to those who are no longer in our lives but continue to bless us: Ami, Abu, Mamoo and Mamma Shehnaz. Miss you.

And finally, thank you, reader. Without you, there would be no book.

Love, always.